YOU COULD

YOU COULD CALL IT MURDER

Lawrence Block

Carroll & Graf Publishers, Inc.
New York

This is for
AMY JO
who was born yesterday.

One

It started at the Tafts, at dinner. All through the meal I had the distinct impression that something more than food was in the offing. The food itself was certainly excellent enough—a fine rare rib roast flanked with roasted potatoes, an excellent red Bordeaux to complement the roast, broccoli au gratin, chef salad with roquefort dressing, all followed up by berry pie, rich strong coffee and snifters of Drambuie. When casual acquaintances invite one in for that sort of meal there's little cause for complaint, but I couldn't help thinking that something was a little out of line.

Perhaps it was the conversation—carefully casual, almost elaborately inoffensive. Perhaps it was the air of repressed urgency that permeated the large dining room. Whatever it was, I was not at all surprised when Edgar Taft called me aside.

"Roy," he said. "Could I talk to you for a minute or two?"

I followed him through the living room to his study, a heavily masculine room with pine-panelled walls and a hunting motif. We sat down in large brown leather chairs. He offered me a cigar. I passed it up and lit a cigarette.

"There's something I wanted to discuss with you, Roy," he said. "I've got a problem. I need your help."

"I thought the dinner was too much to waste merely for the pleasure of my company—"

"Cut it out," he said. "You know I like getting together with you. So does Marianne. But—"

"But you've a problem."

5

He nodded. He stood up abruptly, then began to pace the floor of the study, his eyes troubled. He was a large man, with strong features and firm gray eyes. His hair was iron-gray, his shoulders broad. He was a few years past fifty, but good looks and an almost military carriage took years off his appearance.

He wasn't the sort of man you'd expect to have a problem. Or, if he had one, you'd expect him to solve it himself. He had a great deal of money and he'd made it all by himself. He made his first small fortune years ago as a wildcat well-driller in Texas, doubled that speculating in the stock market, and pyramided those profits by buying control of an unknown electronics corporation, speeding up research and making profits hand over fist. Now, officially, he was retired —but I was relatively certain he had his hands in pies here and there. He was too dynamic to put himself out to pasture.

He turned to me suddenly. "You know my daughter?"

"I met her once," I said. "A tall girl, blonde. I don't remember her name."

"It's Barb. Barbara."

I nodded. "It must have been four years ago when I saw her last," I said. "She was in that awkward stage between girl and young woman, very careful not to trip over her own feet or say the wrong word. But very pretty."

"She's older now," he said grimly. "But still in that awkward stage. And much more beautiful."

"And a problem?"

"And a problem." He ducked the ashes from his cigar, then turned again to face me. "To hell with it, Roy. I might as well come right out and say it. She's missing."

"Missing?"

He nodded. "A missing person," he said. "Whatever that means, exactly. A week ago I got a letter from some old bitch who's the dean of women up at Radbourne. That's a little college in New Hampshire, the place where Barb was going. Letter said Barb had been missing from school for a few days. They wanted to check, find out if she was home, let us know she wasn't there."

"But she wasn't here?"

"Of course not. I got worried as hell, thought somebody

might have snatched her, thought she could have gotten smacked by a car or God knows what. I made a few phone calls to the college and had them check things out. She cashed three big checks the day before she took off, cleaned out her checking account. From there it wasn't too hard to figure."

"I see," I said. "You assume she left on her own?"

"Sure. Hell, she must have. Cleared out with her money and a suitcase full of her clothes. Those checks added up to a little over a thousand dollars, Roy. Not enough to retire on, maybe. But enough to go about as far as she would want to go. You can go around the world on a thousand bucks."

I put out my cigarette. "Why would she want to go?"

"Damned if I know. Hell, maybe she had reasons. She wasn't doing too well in school, according to what they told me. Barb was always a smart kid but she's never been much of a student. She was failing a course or two and not breaking any records in the others. Or it might be some guy—some sharp little bastard who figures on marrying her and cutting himself in on my money. That's why I've been sitting on my hands, figuring I'd hear from her, get a call or a wire saying she's married."

"But that hasn't happened."

He shook his head.

"How old is she, Edgar?"

"Twenty. Twenty-one in March"

"That makes marriage less likely," I told him. "It's December now. You'd think she'd wait until she's twenty-one to marry without consent, especially with only three months to wait."

"I thought of that. But she's impulsive. Hard to figure."

I nodded briefly. "Is the school investigating?"

"Not their job. They checked around town but that's all."

"And you haven't called the police?"

"No."

"Why not?"

He looked at me. "A batch of reasons," he said. "First off, what cops do I call? Radbourne's in some town called Cliff's End. I think it's a ghost town when the college closes shop for the summer. They've got a three-man Mickey Mouse po-

7

lice force straight out of the Keystone Cops. They can't do a hell of a lot. Neither can the New York cops—she isn't here in New York, or if she is there's no way to know about it. The FBI? Hell, it's not a kidnapping. Or if it is, it's a hell of a funny one."

He was right.

"That's not all," he went on. "I'm rich, Roy. Every time I spit one of the tabloids finds room for it. I don't want this in the papers. Maybe it's perfectly innocent, maybe Barb just took off for a week or so and nothing's wrong. But as soon as I yell for the police, Barb's got herself an ugly reputation for a long time. I don't want that."

He paused. "That's why I called you," he said. "I'm scared to pick out an ordinary private detective. I've used plenty of them in my business and I know which ones you can trust. Even the big agencies have operatives who talk too damned much. And you never know when one of their boys is going to hit a situation with blackmail potential and open up shop for himself. I need a friend, somebody I can trust all the way."

"And you want me to find her?"

"That's it."

I thought about it. It's no easy matter to turn up a missing person, harder still when that person could be almost any place in the country, not to say the world. The needle in the haystack analogy had never fit more perfectly.

"I don't know what I can accomplish, Edgar. But I'll be glad to do what I can."

"That's all I want," he said. He sat down at his desk and opened a drawer, took out a checkbook. He uncapped a pen, filled out a check in a hurry, tore it from the book and handed it to me. "This is a retainer, Roy. Anytime you want more dough, all you have to do is ask for it. I don't care what this costs me. The money doesn't make a hell of a difference. I just want to have Barb back, to know that nothing's wrong with her."

I took the check, glanced at it. It was made payable to Roy Markham in the amount of ten thousand dollars. It was signed Edgar Taft. I folded it twice and gave it a temporary home in my billfold.

8

"That enough?"

"More than enough," I said honestly. "I—"

"You need more, just yell. Don't worry how high your expenses go. I'm not going to worry about them. Just do what you can."

"I'll need information."

"I'll give you what I can, Roy."

"Pictures would help," I said. "For a starter. It's been awhile since I saw Barbara."

He was nodding. He opened the same desk drawer again and took out a plain white envelope. He passed it to me. "These are the recent ones," he said. "All within the past two or three years. She doesn't take a good picture but they're not too bad."

I opened the envelope, took out a handful of snapshots. The girl in the photographs was a prettier one than I remembered. She was becoming a very beautiful woman. Her forehead was broad and intelligent, her mouth full, her hair long and light and lovely.

"These will help," I said.

"What next?"

The next question was harder. "How do you get along with her, Edgar? Are you . . . close? Friendly?"

"She's my daughter."

"I know that. Are you on good terms?"

He frowned, then looked away. "Not good terms," he said. "Not bad terms either. I've spent a lot of time making money, Roy. Almost all my time. It's the only thing I know. I'm not highly educated, don't read books, can't stand high society and fancy parties. I'm a businessman and it's all I know. I suppose I should have learned to be a family man somewhere along the line. I didn't."

I waited.

"I never spent much time with Barb. God knows she had everything she ever wanted—clothes, money, a trip to Europe last year, expensive schooling, the works. But not too much closeness, damn it. And it shows."

"How?"

"We don't get along," he said. "Oh, we don't throw rocks at each other or anything. But we don't get along. She thinks

I'm a dull old man who pays the bills. Period. She's a hell of a lot closer with Marianne than with me. But she doesn't take Marianne into her confidence either. She keeps a lot to herself."

He paused. "Maybe that's why I don't have any idea where she is now. Or what she's up to. Maybe that's why I'm a lot more scared about this business than I should be. Hell, I don't know. She's a funny kid, Roy."

"Has she ever been in trouble?"

"Not . . . not really."

"What does that mean?"

He thought it over. "It means what I said," he said finally. "She's never been in any real trouble. But she travels with a pretty fast crowd, Roy. A bunch of kids like her, kids with more money than they should have. You know, when I was a kid my old man had a pot and a window and that was all. A pot to crap in and a window to throw it out of. That's supposed to turn a kid into a criminal, right?"

"Sometimes."

"With me it worked the other way. I looked around and I told myself that, dammit to hell, I was going to have better than this for myself. I never got through high school. I dropped out and took a job working twelve hours a day six days a week. I banked my money so I'd something to work with, some capital to play around with. Then I looked for the right long shots and backed them all the way. I started with nothing and I came out of it with a pile."

"And it's the other way with Barbara?"

"Maybe. Hell, I don't know exactly what I'm trying to say. Her crowd has too much dough. She gets a big allowance and spends every penny of it, wouldn't dream of saving a nickel. She knows there's more waiting for her. She drives her car too damn fast. She goes out with guys who drink too damn much. She stays out too late. Maybe she sleeps around. They say all college girls sleep around. You know anything about it?"

"They're too young for me."

He didn't smile. "Sometimes I worry," he said. "Maybe I don't worry enough. I can't talk to her about it, can't talk to her about a damn thing. Whenever I try talking to her she goes off the handle and we have a little fireworks. We yell at each other for awhile. Oh, to hell with it. I want you to find Barb, Roy. I want you to bring her back here. That's all I can say."

I asked several more questions but his answers weren't of much help. He didn't know the names of any of her friends at Radbourne, didn't know of any man or boy she had been seeing on a steady basis. I suggested that his wife might be able to help.

"Uh-uh," he said. "I've been over this with Marianne a dozen times already. I know everything she knows."

"That's not too much."

"I know it," he said. "Hell, I know it. Will you do what you can?"

"Of course."

We shook hands on it, more or less to seal the bargain that had already been made the moment I took his check. The interview was over. He led me out of his study into the living room. Marianne was waiting for us.

She was a sweet, frail woman with quiet gray hair and trusting puppy-eyes. She was the sort of person whom no one swore in front of. I had always had the impression that she was much stronger inside than anyone suspected.

"Roy's going to help us," Taft said.

Marianne smiled. "I'm glad," she said softly. "You'll find Barb, won't you, Roy?"

I said I would try.

"Of course you'll find her," she said, blandly dismissing the possibility of failure. "I'm so glad you'll be helping us. Call us as soon as you find Barb, won't you?"

I told her I would. I thanked her for dinner and told her very truthfully that it had been a marvellous meal. Then Edgar Taft walked me out of the house and down the long sloping driveway. His car was parked in front.

"No car," he said. "How come? You don't like to drive in New York?"

"I had a car for awhile," I told him. "I got rid of it."

He looked at me. "It would be in New York and I would be in San Francisco," I explained. "Or it would be in San Francisco and I would be in London. It never quite managed to catch up with me. So I decided I would get along without it."

"You still do that much travelling?"

I nodded. "I like to keep on the move," I said. "I still maintain my brownstone in the east sixties but I'm hardly ever there. Right now I'm staying at the Commodore."

"I called your office—"

"You called my answering service," I said. "My office is my suitcase. I've only been in New York a week. And I guess I won't be here much longer."

"Well," he said. "Hop in. I'll run you down to the station."

The Taft home was in Bedford Hills, a wealthy estate section in upper Westchester County. The house was a huge Dutch colonial with a view of the Hudson. Ancient trees shaded the rolling lawn. I got into the front seat of his Lincoln and we drove off.

We talked about odds and ends for part of the trip. Then, as we were nearing the railroad station, he asked me where I was going to start.

"There only seems to be one place," I said. "I'll have to begin at the college. Radbourne. What did you say the name of the town was?"

. "Cliff's End. Cliff's End, New Hampshire."

It sounded desolate enough. I asked him if any trains went there. He said he didn't know, that Barbara always drove up. She had a red MG sports roadster. The license number was written on the back of one of the snapshots he had given me.

"Keep in touch with me," he said at the station. "Call me collect once a day. After dinner's the best time to catch me. Hell, Barb might turn up any minute. I wouldn't want you wasting your time."

"I'll call you."

"Fine," he said. "Do your best, Roy." He checked his watch. "The next New York train should be through in fifteen minutes or so. Luck."

I shook hands with him. His grip was firm. Then I walked to the railway platform and looked back, watching the Lincoln drive off. I lighted a cigarette and waited for the train to come.

12

The platform was empty of others. I stood smoking and thought about Edgar Taft and his errant daughter. Something refused to jibe, something was inconsistent. I couldn't pin it down offhand—I could only realize for certain that things were not entirely as they seemed to be.

Which, in American terminology, was the way the ball bounced, the way the tootsie rolled. *Sic friat crustulum,* as they might put it in Rome. Thus crumbles the cookie.

The train came and I boarded it. It was a rolling antique but its seats were comfortable. I sat in one of them, took a paperbound book from my back pocket, and read some verses of Catullus until the poor old train managed to haul itself into Grand Central.

I closed the book, left the train. I walked upstairs and into the Commodore lobby, then took an elevator to the fourteenth floor. It would have been the thirteenth floor, but for a rather bizarre American custom of eliminating that floor from the overall scheme of things.

The bellhop brought me a pint of scotch and a bottle of white soda. I put some of each into a glass and worked on the mixture, with a half dozen pictures of Barbara Taft spread out in front of me. I looked at the pictures and tried to figure out a way to find the girl.

It would not be easy.

She had a car and she had a sizeable bankroll, and with either of the two she could put a great distance between herself and the town of Cliff's End. I wondered if she was simply taking a week or two off. Edgar Taft had said she was a girl who ran with a wild crowd; if that were so, it didn't seem unlikely that she might decide to run off from school on a lark.

And, if that were so, why was he so worried?

There were more questions than there were answers. I took a hot bath and let muscles loosen up and tension float away. I dried off, combined a little more scotch with a little more soda, and got into bed. The bellhop had also brought ice cubes, for no good reason. I prefer the British custom of taking liquor at room temperature, a source of never-ending amusement to Americans. Ice kills the taste.

It had been a long day. I put the snapshots of Barbara

13

Taft in my wallet, took out Edgar's check, looked at it reverently. I endorsed it over to my bank, stuck it in a bank-by-mail envelope, and dropped it in the mail chute in the hall. Then I went back to my room and finished my drink and got into bed.

Sleep came quickly.

Two

CLIFF'S END is an elusive destination. First you ride the New York Central to Boston. You wait there for an hour or so, then change to a railroad called, strangely, the Massachusetts Northern. This leaves you in a hamlet known as Byington, New Hampshire. There, after a wait of another pair of hours, you board a bus which eventually drops you in Cliff's End.

I did this. The ride—or rides, really—was at least as bad as it sounds. Perhaps worse. It was late afternoon when I left the bus in Cliff's End, deposited without ceremony at the main intersection of the town in knee-deep snow. I lit a cigarette and started looking for the college.

It wasn't difficult to find, since there wasn't much more to the town. Girls with pony tails and boys with crew cuts hurried in all directions. Boys threw snowballs at girls. Girls ducked and giggled, or giggled and ducked. I asked one where the Administration Building was. She pointed vaguely to my left. It was a tactical error, because a callow youth promptly beaned her with a snowball. She giggled anyway.

I left her giggling and found the Administration Building more or less on my own. It was a large brick Gothic affair with huge and apparently pointless towers rising at either end into the blue sky. I went inside and had someone show me where the dean of women had her office. Her name, it turned out, was Helen MacIlhenny. I introduced myself and she beamed at me.

"Sit down, Mr. Markham," she said. "Mr. Taft called me

this morning. He said you'd be up sometime today and asked me to help you as much as possible. I'll be glad to."

She was nearly sixty and still growing old gracefully. Her black hair was only slightly salted with gray and her eyes were chunks of flint in a taut, keen face. She had a wedding ring on her ring finger and a fragile gold brooch on the front of her suit jacket. She smiled nicely.

"Now I'm not too sure what help I can give you," she said. "I told Mr. Taft as much as I knew. I don't know that much, Mr. Markham. Barbara simply disappeared. One day she was here and the next day she was not."

"When was she last seen?"

"Let me see . . . today is Thursday, isn't it? Barbara missed all her classes a week ago Tuesday. She attended an eleven o'clock French class Monday morning. No one has seen her since then."

"Then she could have left any time after noon on Monday?"

"That's right."

"Was she sharing a room with another girl?"

Helen MacIlhenny nodded. "The girl's name is Gwen Davison. Her room is in Lockesley Hall—Room 304. I'm sure she'll cooperate to the best of her ability."

"Was she a close friend of Barbara's?"

"No—that's why she'll cooperate." The dean's eyes twinkled at me. "I can't imagine a less likely pair than Barbara and Gwen, Mr. Markham. Gwen is the perfect student, in a sense. She's not brilliant, never the shining star, but she does her work thoroughly and has maintained a B-plus average for three years now. Never in trouble, never emotionally upset."

"And Barbara's not like that?"

"Hardly. Do you know her?"

I shook my head.

"Barbara," she said, "is not the perfect student."

"I gathered as much."

"Yet in a sense she's a more rewarding individual, Mr. Markham. She's a very deep person, a profound person. She's subject to fits of depression that seem almost psychotic in their intensity. She will throw herself into a subject which

16

interests her to the exclusion of all other subjects. She feels things deeply and reacts very dramatically. She falls in and out of love frequently. Is a picture beginning to emerge?"

"I think so."

She leaned forward and fixed her eyes upon me. "It's hard for me to find words for this. The girl's dynamic—you have to know her to understand her. She's not an easy girl to handle. But I have the feeling that she's worth the effort, if you follow me. There's a great deal of potential there, a lot of personality. She could turn into a spectacular person."

I switched the subject. "Where do you think she is?"

"I have no idea."

"Do you think she went to get married?"

She pursed her lips and considered it. "It's possible, Mr. Markham. The runaway marriage is always a possibility on any college campus. If it's the case, she's not marrying a Radbourne boy."

"None missing?"

"None. But she could have married someone else, of course. Someone from another college. Someone from New York."

"What do you think?"

"I doubt it."

"Why?"

Her eyes narrowed. "I didn't tell this to Mr. Taft," she said. "I didn't want to set him on edge. According to what I've learned so far, Barbara was in some kind of trouble."

"How do you mean?"

"I wish I knew. She may have been pregnant but I somehow doubt it. A few girls have mentioned that she was acting nervous lately, just before she disappeared. Nervous and withdrawn and tense. Worried about something and not saying what."

I said, "Pregnant—"

"It happens in the best of families, Mr. Markham. And in the best colleges."

"But you don't think it happened to Barbara?"

"I don't. Frankly, I don't think it would have worried her that much. That seems odd, doesn't it? But I suspect Barbara would simply have found herself a good abortionist and

17

had an abortion. And would have returned without missing a single class that she didn't want to miss."

I switched the subject again. "Was she going with any boys in particular?"

"With several. Lately she was dating a boy named Alan Marsten. I've talked to him and he says he knows nothing about Barbara's disappearance. You might want to talk to him."

I wrote the name down. "That's all I can think of," she said, rising. "If there are any other questions—"

I told her I couldn't think of any myself.

"I have an appointment, then, which I might as well keep. You have the run of the campus, of course. And if there's anything more, please call me. Will you be staying in Cliff's End overnight?"

"I might be."

"You'll probably have to," she told me. "The last bus passes through in an hour and a half and you'll be here longer than that, won't you?" She didn't wait for an answer. "Mrs. Lipton rents rooms by the day and keeps a nice home. The address is 504 Phillips Street. I understand the rates are reasonable enough. For meals you might try either the school cafeteria or the tavern in town. I recommend the tavern. It's been a pleasure, Mr. Markham."

I followed her out of her office, waited while she locked the door with a small brass key. Together we walked out the front entrance of the big building.

"It must be interesting to be a detective," she said idly. "Do you enjoy it?"

"I enjoy it."

"I suspect it's a little like being a dean," she said thoughtfully. "You'll want to see Gwen Davison now, no doubt. Lockesley Hall is that way—the three-story brick building along that path. Yes, that's the one. Good luck, Mr. Markham."

I stood for a moment and stared after her. Her stride was firm and she moved along with surprising speed for a woman her age. Her mind was even faster.

I turned and trudged off through the snow.

18

I had the wrong mental picture of Gwen Davison. I went to Room 304 of Lockesley Hall expecting to meet up with a round-faced and sexless creature wearing tortoise-shell glasses and a frozen stare. She was not like that at all.

In the first place, she was pretty. Her hair was jet black, curling in little ringlets. Her complexion had sprung full-blown from a soap advertisement and her figure from a bra advertisement. Young breasts strained against the front of a pale blue cashmere sweater. Warm brown eyes measured me and held approval in abeyance for the time being.

I revised my estimate of her. I'd expected a frigid student and she was not that at all. She was, instead, the perfect American coed. She was the girl who played everything by one book or another, who would play sex by the marriage manual and life by Norman Vincent Peale, who would marry a company man and have two-point-seven children.

"I don't know where Barb is," she said. "I don't know what happened to her. I bet she deserved it, whatever it is."

"You don't like her?"

She shrugged. "I don't like her or dislike her. We had nothing in common but this room." She gestured around. The room they had in common was nothing to go into ecstasies over. There were four walls and a ceiling and a floor, with the usual amount of dormitory furniture. It did not look like the sort of place somebody would want to live in.

"And she was no bargain to room with," she went on. "She was a pill. She would come at five in the morning, turning on lights and banging doors and raising hell. She'd drink too much and heave it up in the sink. She was a real pleasure, believe me."

"When did you see her last?"

"Monday morning."

"Not since then?"

"No. Somebody said she went to her eleven o'clock class. I don't know for sure. But she didn't stay here Monday night."

"Did you report it?"

"Of course not." She gave me an odd look. "Listen, I didn't like Barb. I told you, she's a pill. I can live without her. But if she wants to spend a night somewhere that's her business."

19

"Has she done that before?"

She let that one pass. "When I didn't see her for two nights I called the dean. I thought something might have have happened to her. That's all."

I asked her if she cared if I smoked. She didn't. I lighted a cigarette and blew a cloud of smoke at the ceiling. I tried to concentrate. It didn't work.

I wasn't getting anywhere. I wasn't even getting pointed in the right direction. All I knew was that Barbara wasn't on campus, which was something I managed to guess a long while back. The dean of women liked her but disapproved of her, her roommate neither liked nor approved of her, and I didn't know where in God's good name she was.

A puzzle.

"Did she take her car?"

"Naturally," Gwen Davison said. "Anybody with a car like that one would take it along."

"And her clothes?"

"Just a suitcase full. She left more clothes than I own. Wouldn't you know she's two sizes bigger than I am?"

I looked at the dark-haired girl, glanced at the front of her sweater. I was willing to bet that a certain portion of Barbara's anatomy was not two sizes larger than Gwen's. It was simply a biological impossibility.

"I'd like to look through Barbara's clothes," I said. "And her desk and books. If it's all right with you."

"I don't care," she said. "Just leave everything like you find it. That's all."

She took that as a signal to ignore me. She picked up a book—a sociology textbook—and buried her face in it. I went over to Barbara's desk and started to open drawers and look through papers. It was a waste of time.

There were letters and papers. The letters were all from home, all from Marianne, and they were all bright and cheerful and insipid. The papers were mostly notes of one sort or another, scraps of poetry that Barbara had been working on, random lecture notes. They were arranged in no particular order.

I looked through her dresser, feeling rather like a Peeping Tom as I went through mounds of undergarments. I checked

20

her closet and came up with nothing. I learned a few things, but they all seemed to be things I had already known.

"Gwen—"

She turned to look at me.

"She left in a hurry," I said. "She threw a few articles of clothing into a suitcase and hurried off. And that's puzzling. Dean MacIlhenny said that Barbara has been nervous lately. I'd expect that she would have been planning to leave, would have taken the time to pack everything. But she left almost all her clothing behind. It's as though she ran off on an impulse."

"She's an impulsive girl."

"What do you think happened?"

She thought it over. "I think something was worrying her. She gets depressed every once in a while and sits around the room moping. She was doing that. And she got a little hysterical, if you know what I mean. You know—laughing very shrill and short over nothing at all, pacing the floor like a caged lion. It was getting tough to live with her."

"And you think she just left on the spur of the moment?"

"I told you before," she said. "I don't know what she did and I don't care. But if I had to guess, that's what I would say. I think she grabbed a suitcase and hopped in that hot little car of hers and took off for awhile. Then she got involved in something and forgot to come back. You know what's going to happen next?"

"What?"

"She'll come back," she said positively. "She'll come back in her flashy car with her suitcase in her hand and a smile on her face and she'll expect everyone to hug her and kiss her and welcome her with open arms. She's in for a shock, I'm afraid."

"Why?"

"Because this is a little too much," Gwen Davison told me. "You can't disappear for a week and a half without a word. They'll throw her out of Radbourne for this one." She frowned. "Not that it should matter to Barb. What does she need with a college degree? With her father's money she can buy herself an honorary degree if she wants. She's fixed for life with or without college. So why should she care?"

21

We talked for a few more minutes but I didn't get anything more from the girl. The only boy friend of Barbara's she knew of was the one Helen MacIlhenny had mentioned, Alan Marsten. She didn't care for him either.

"One of the Bohemian element," she said. "You know the kind. He never wears anything but paint-spattered dungarees and a dirty sweatshirt. Gets his hair cut once every six months. Sits around looking romantic and artistic. You can usually find him hanging around at the little coffee shop in town. It's called Grape Leaves. God knows why."

I thanked her and left. It was colder outside now and the sky was darker. Now it was snowing again, the flakes drifting down slowly through crisp air. I pulled up my coat collar, lit a cigarette, and headed toward town.

The streets of Cliff's End were cold and uninviting. Without the college, the town would have been a typical tiny New England village, a cluster of low buildings grouped around the inevitable village square with its inevitable colonial courthouse. The college changed this, and while it may have greatly enhanced the prosperity of the region, that was about all it did on the plus side. The stores aimed their displays at the student trade. The villagers sat on their stoops, rocking endlessly and mumbling mean things about the collegians. It was a cold little town, and the snow was only partially responsible for the coldness.

I found Grape Leaves across the street from the tavern. It was closed; a hand-lettered sign in the window announced that it would open in an hour or so. I crossed the street to the tavern, remembering all at once that I hadn't had anything resembling a meal since breakfast. The sandwiches I wolfed down in various bus and train stations had been little but a hedge against starvation. Now I was ravenous.

The tavern was English in decor and had me momentarily homesick for London. I sat on a hard wooden chair at an old wooden table and ordered a mug of ale as a starter. An aproned student brought me the ale in a pewter mug with a thick glass bottom. It was full-bodied and delicious.

The food didn't quite match the ale but it was better than I had expected. I had a small steak with onions and a baked potato with another mug of ale to keep them company. The two ales had my head a little fuzzy and I cleared things up with a pot of black coffee.

By the time I left the tavern, lights were on in the coffee house across the street. I went over, swung open a door and went inside. The place was furnished in imitation Greenwich Village, which may be a redundant description. Candles dripped over chianti bottles on the small tables. A handful of students, most of them the worse for wear, were draped over tables, lost either in conversation or thought or whatever esoteric reveries were provided by the paperbound books they were reading. A waiter asked me what I wanted. When I told him I was looking for Alan Marsten he pointed to a boy about twenty slouching over a small cup of coffee at a table set against one wall. Then he turned away and ignored me.

I went over, sat opposite Alan Marsten. He looked up, stared blankly at me, then went back to his coffee. Moments later he looked up again.

"You're still here," he said slowly. "I thought maybe you'd go away."

"You're Alan Marsten?"

"Why?"

He was wearing the uniform Gwen Davison had described —blue denim trousers spattered with various hues of paint, a sweatshirt similarly decorated, a pair of dirty chukka boots. His hair was long and needed combing. He could have used a shave.

"I want to talk with you," I said. "About Barbara Taft."

"Go to hell."

The words were venomous. He fixed watery blue eyes on me and hated me with them. His fists were clenched on the table top.

"Who are you, man?"

"Roy Markham," I said.

"It's a name, I guess. Who sent you?"

"Edgar Taft. Barbara's father."

He snorted at me. "So the old man is starting to sweat. Well, he's got it coming. You tell him he can go to hell for himself, will you? What does he want?"

I looked at him and tried to guess what Barbara could have seen in him. His features were good except for a weak

23

mouth and chin. I wondered what he thought he was—hipster or beatnik or angry young man. I decided he was just a slovenly kid.

"Barbara's missing," I said. "He's worried about her. He wants to know where she is."

"So do I."

"You don't know?"

He looked at me carefully. "I don't," he said. "If I did, I wouldn't tell you. I wouldn't tell anybody."

"Why not?"

"Because it's Barb's business what she does. She's a big girl now, man. She can take care of herself."

"Maybe she's in trouble."

"Maybe."

"Is she?"

His eyes mocked me. "I told you," he said. Barb's a big girl. She can take care of herself. What's your bit, anyway? You some kind of a cop?"

"I'm a private investigator."

"I'll be a son of a bitch. The old man's got private eyes looking for her. Somebody oughta shoot him."

He was getting on my nerves. "You take quite an interest in all this, don't you?"

"Maybe."

"Why? Was she paying your bills for you?"

"Don't let the clothes fool you," he snapped. "My old man's just as loaded as Barb's. And just as much of a bastard."

I wasn't getting very far. I lighted a cigarette and smoked, waiting for him to say something else. A girl with long black hair and too much lipstick asked me what I wanted to order. I asked for coffee and she brought me a demitasse cup of it. It was black and bitter and it cost me a quarter.

"What the hell," he said finally. "I couldn't tell you anything even if I wanted to. I don't know where she went."

"She left without telling you?"

He nodded. "I wasn't surprised. Something's been bugging her. She's in trouble, bad trouble."

"What kind of trouble?"

He shrugged. "There's all kinds. Money trouble, man trou-

24

ble, pregnant trouble, school trouble, sadness trouble. I don't think it was money—her old man gives her enough bread, even if he doesn't show her anything else. I don't think she was pregnant—"

"Were you sleeping with her?"

"None of your business," he said, angry now. "What I do is my business. What Barb does is her business."

Which could mean anything, I decided. "You love her?"

His eyes clouded. "Maybe. Big word, love. She's gone, maybe she's coming back, maybe she isn't. I don't know."

I asked him a few more questions and he didn't have answers for them. He said he didn't know why she had left or where she might have gone, didn't know anyone likely to be able or willing to supply any of the answers. I wasn't sure whether or not he was telling the truth. I had a hunch he knew more than he was ready to tell me, but there wasn't much I could do about it.

I finished my cigarette. There were no ashtrays; I dropped the butt to the bare wooden floor and squashed it with my foot. I left the coffee there. The management was welcome to reheat it and collect another quarter for it.

And I left Grape Leaves.

It was close to eight. I found a drugstore, changed a pair of dollars for the telephone booth. The pharmacist had heavily lidded eyes and dirty hands. I wondered how many contraceptives he sold to Radbourne students.

I shut myself up in the phone booth, put a dime in the slot and managed to convince the operator that I wished to call Bedford Hills, New York. I didn't bother trying to get her to make the call collect as Edgar Taft had suggested. It would have been too much trouble.

Instead I poured nickels and dimes and quarters into the telephone until the woman was satisfied. After an annoying delay a phone started to ring. Someone picked it up midway through the first ring and barked hello at me.

I asked for Taft.

"Who's this?"

"Roy Markham," I said.

25

"Markham," the voice said. "You the private eye that Taft sent to look for his daughter?"

"That's right."

"You can quit looking."

"Who's this?"

"Hanovan," the voice said. "Homicide. We found the girl in the Hudson, Markham. It looks like suicide."

I said: "God."

"Yeah. It was messy. It's always messy. She spent a few days floating and they don't look too beautiful after a few days in the river. They never look beautiful dead."

I didn't say anything.

"I guess that's it," he said. "But you don't have to look for her any more."

"Can I speak with Mr. Taft?"

"I don't know, Markham. He's pretty broken up. We had a doc come over and give his wife a sedative, put her to sleep for awhile. But Taft—"

I heard noises in the background. Then Taft's voice, loud, came over the wire.

"Is that Roy Markham? Gimme the phone, damn it. Let me talk to him."

Somebody must have given him the phone. He said: "It's terrible, Roy. God, it's awful."

I didn't know what to say or whether I was supposed to say anything at all. He didn't give me time to worry about it. "Get right back to New York," he said. "Come up here right away. These cops think she killed herself. I don't believe it, Roy. Barb wouldn't do a thing like that."

"Well—"

"You get here as soon as you can," he went on. "Somebody murdered my daughter, Roy. I want that killer. I want you to find him and I want to see him go to the chair. I want to watch him die, Roy."

I didn't say anything. I looked through the phone booth's glass door. The pharmacist was busy counting pills. A pair of students near the front of the store were leafing through a display of magazines.

26

"Roy? You're coming?"

I let out my breath and realized that I had been holding it for a long while.

"I'm coming," I said. "I'll be there as soon as I can."

Three

I FOUND a mercenary student with an ancient Packard and bribed a ride to Byington. The buses weren't running and I can't say I blamed them. Snow carpeted the roads while wind blew more snow across the road at us. But the old car was tough as nails, built for rough weather and bad roads, and the boy knew how to drive. He got me to Byington in far less time than the bus would have taken, pocketed his bribe with a huge smile, turned the Packard around and aimed it at Cliff's End once again. Less than twenty minutes passed before the Massachusetts Northern came to take me to Boston. I picked up the Central there and rode it to New York, then got off it and onto another which carried me back up the Hudson Valley as far as Bedford Hills. I called the Taft home from a pay-phone in the station—it was late and no cabs were handy. The policeman who said his name was Hanovan answered and told me he'd send a car around for me. I waited until an unmarked black Ford pulled up and a hand waved at me.

I went over to the car, got into it. The man behind the wheel was wearing a rumpled gray business suit. His hair was black, his nose broad, his eyes tired. I asked him if Hanovan had sent him.

"I'm Hanovan," he said. "So you're Markham. I was talking to Bill Runyon about you. He said you're all right."

"I worked with him once."

"He told me." He took out a cigarette and lighted one without offering me the pack. I lighted one of my own and drew smoke into my lungs. The car's motor was running but we were still at the curb. I wondered what we were waiting for.

"I wanted to talk to you," he said. "Without Taft listening. That's why I stayed around his place. There's nothing to do there but I wanted to talk to you."

I said nothing.

"The kid killed herself," he said. "No question about it. We fished her out of the Hudson around Pier Eighty-one—that's the Hudson Day Line slot near Forty-second Street. Death was by drowning—no bumps on the head, no bullet holes, nothing. She took a jump in the drink and drowned."

I swallowed. "How long had she been dead?"

"That's hard to say, Markham. You leave somebody in the water more than two days, you can't tell too much. The doc says she was in for three days minimum. Maybe as many as five." He shrugged heroically. "That's as close as he would make it. Look, let me tell you what we got. The way we figure it, she hit the water from one of the piers between Fifty-ninth Street and Forty-second. Her car turned up in a garage on West Fifty-third between Eighth and Ninth. It's been there since late Monday night and the guy we talked to didn't remember anything about who parked it. That fits the time, Markham. It's Thursday night now. That would be four days in the water, which checks with what the medical examiner guessed."

I nodded.

"We figured she garaged the car and went for a walk. The docks are empty that time of night. She walked out on a pier, took off her clothes—"

"She was naked when you found her?"

He nodded emphatically. "Suicides usually work that way. The ones who go for a swim, anyways. They take everything off and fold it up neat and then go and jump."

"Did you find her clothes?"

"Nope. Which is no surprise, if you stop and think about it. You leave something on a pier and you're not going to find it three days later. She was a rich kid, wore expensive clothes. Somewhere a longshoreman's got a wife or girl-friend with a pretty new dress."

"Go on."

29

He turned his hands palms-up. "Go where? That does it, Markham. Look, she went and she jumped. Period. She was a moody kid and she wasn't doing well in school. So she took what looked like an easy out, turned herself into a floater. It happens all the time. It's not nice, it doesn't look pretty or smell sweet. But it happens all the time."

"Was she pregnant?"

He shook his head. "We checked, of course. She wasn't. That's why a lot of 'em go swimming. Not this one."

I dragged on the cigarette and watched him out of the corner of an eye. He seemed perfectly at ease, a rational man explaining a situation in a straightforward manner. I rolled down the side window and dropped my cigarette to the ground. I turned around and looked at him again.

"Why?"

He looked back at me. "Why did she kill herself? Hell, I don't know. She probably—"

"That's not what I mean. Why give me such an elaborate build-up? I'm not your superior. You don't owe me a report or a favor. Why tell me all this?"

He colored. "I was just trying to help you out."

"I'm sure you were. Why?"

He studied his own cigarette. It had burned almost to his fingertips. "Look," he said. "This girl—Taft's daughter—killed herself. I know it. You know it. Even Taft's wife knows it."

"But Taft doesn't?"

"You guessed it." He sighed heavily. "Now ordinarily if a suicide's old man wants to make noise, I just nod and gentle him and then leave him alone. I don't sit and hold his hand all night long. The hell, I'm a New York City cop and this is Westchester. Why worry about him?"

I didn't say anything.

"This is different, Markham. Taft is rich. He knows a lot of people, throws a lot of weight. I can't tell him he's full of crap, can't brush him off. I have to be nice."

"And you want me to tell him she killed herself?"

"Wrong." He put out the cigarette. "He wants you to investigate," he said. "I told him we'd follow it up but he doesn't have any faith in us, mainly because I already told

30

him how sure I am that it's suicide all the way. What I want is for you to tell him you'll work on it, you're not too sold on the suicide bit yourself. Then you move into the case."

"And look for a mythical killer?"

"I don't give a damn if you sit on your hands, Markham. I want you to make like you're working like a Turk. Gradually you can't find anything. Gradually he wakes up and realizes what I been trying to tell him all along. Gradually he sees it's suicide. And in the meantime he stays off my back."

I didn't say anthing. He asked me if I got it, and I told him that I got it, all right. I didn't like it.

I didn't enjoy the notion of wasting my time and Edgar Taft's money just to do the New York police a favor. I didn't enjoy the "gradual" routine—a gradual let-down of Edgar Taft, a gradual change in tone.

"You'll do it, Markham?" I didn't answer him. "Look at it this way. You'll be doing the old man a favor. Right now he's all broken up. He can't stand believing any daughter of his knocked herself off. It's a big thing with him. Okay—so you got to let him believe somebody killed her. And he wants action. So you give him what he thinks is action until his mind gets used to the idea of what really happened. It makes things a lot easier for a lot of people, Markham. I'm one of them. I admit it. But it makes it easier for Taft, too."

"All right," I said.

"You'll go along with it?"

"I said I would," I told him, my voice tired now. "Now why don't you try shutting your mouth and driving?"

He looked at me and thought it over. Then he put the car in gear and stepped down heavily on the gas pedal. Neither of us said a word on the way to Taft's house.

Edgar Taft was crushed but strong, broken but surprisingly firm. He didn't rant, didn't rave, didn't foam at the mouth. Instead he talked in a painfully placid voice, explaining very earnestly to me that the police were a bunch of fools, that deep down inside he knew Barbara as he knew himself, that she couldn't kill herself any more than he could.

"A batch of damn fools, Roy. They couldn't find crap in a

31

latrine, not even if you took them and stuck their heads down the holes. I'm giving you full authority and all expenses. I'm telling them to cooperate with you. That's one nice thing about money, Roy. If I tell them to cooperate with you they'll let you do any damn thing you want. Roy—"

There was more. But it was all in the same vein, all stamped from the same mold. What it boiled down to was that he wanted me to find his daughter's murderer. That was all there was to it. I let him know that it was a tall order, agreed that the police were being far too quick to write the case off as suicide, and told him I'd do what I could.

Marianne was different, though.

She was as well-mannered as ever, as neat and sweet and soft-spoken as she had always been. She was the gracious lady, accepting reality and greeting it with decorum, maintaining her posistion and being what she was supposed to be.

"Roy," she said. "I'm . . . I'm very glad to see you, Roy. This is all very hard for me. My daughter committed suicide, Roy. Barb killed herself, jumped into the water and drowned herself. This is hard for me."

It was hard but she was handling it nicely. I had always thought of her as a person with internal strength and now she was proving me correct. I took her arm. We found a sofa and sat side-by-side on it. I lighted cigarettes for us both.

"Poor Edgar," she said. "He can't believe it, you know. He'll scream at imaginary killers forever."

"And you?"

Her eyes clouded. "Maybe I'm more realistic," she said. "I . . . I was afraid this had happened . . . or would happen . . . from the moment we found out she had left school. I think I got my tenses scrambled in that sentence, Roy."

"I wouldn't worry about it. Edgar says Barbara wasn't the type of girl to commit suicide."

"Edgar is wrong."

"He is?"

She nodded. "He's wrong," she said again. "He has never understood her, not really."

"He says he knows her as he knows himself."

That brought a smile. A joyless one. "Perhaps he does,"

32

she half whispered. "Or did. Because there's very little left to know now, is there?"

"Marianne—"

"I'm all right, Roy. Really, I'm all right. To get back to what I was saying—Edgar and Barbara were very much alike. She was the same sort of person. Maybe that's why they fought so much. I used to think so."

I looked at her. "He wouldn't choose suicide, Marianne."

"You think not?" Her eyes were amazingly firm. "He's never failed, Roy. He's never had any reason to kill himself. Barb evidently failed, or thought she did. I suppose it amounts to the same thing, doesn't it?"

Hanovan drove me back to New York. He turned on the radio and we listened to some sort of teen age craze playing a guitar and groaning horribly. I suppose it served its purpose —at least Hanovan and I were relieved of the necessity of speaking to one another, which was fortunate.

Actually, I had no reason to dislike him. In a sense he was advising a course of action which was probably the best thing all around for the people involved. Naturally it made his life a great deal simpler, but it also made for a psychological solution to Edgar Taft's traumas.

I managed to ignore both Hanovan and the ersatz music until he let me out of the car at Times Square. I was exhausted without being sleepy. I was as hungry as I was tired— the small steak at the tavern in Cliff's End had been far too small, and far too long ago. I found an all-night restaurant, went in and sat down. A waitress brought me a mushroom omelet with home fries and a cup of black coffee. I ate the omelet and the potatoes and tried not to listen to a juke box which gave forth with the same sort of pseudo music I'd tried not to listen to in Hanovan's car. I drank the coffee, smoked a cigarette.

Outside on 42nd Street it was cold. Not so cold as the humble hamlet of Cliff's End, but cold enough to make me give up the idea of walking across town to the Commodore. The wind had a snap to it and my breath smoked in the cold air. I stepped to the curb and flagged down a taxi.

He pulled over. I opened the door, stepped inside. I muttered *Commodore* at the husky driver and started to close the door. Then all at once somebody was yanking it open again and piling into the cab with me.

"You've got to help me!"

The somebody was a girl. Her hair was black and short, her eyes large and frightened. She was struggling to catch her breath and it seemed to be a lost cause.

I asked her what the matter was. She tried to tell me, opened her mouth without getting any words out, then whirled in her seat and pointed. I followed the direction of the point. Two grim characters, short and dark and ugly, were grabbing a cab of their own.

"After me," she stammered. "Trying to kill me. Oh, help me, for God's sake!"

The driver was staring at us and wondering what in God's name was happening. I couldn't say I blamed him. I was wondering pretty much the same thing myself.

"Just drive," I told him.

"You still want the Commodore?"

"No," I said. "Just drive around. We'll see what happens."

He drove around while I saw what happened. He turned downtown on Broadway, held Broadway to 36th Street, headed east on 36th as far as Madison, then swung north again. I kept one eye on the girl and the other gazing out through the rear window. The girl stayed in her seat and the cab with the two grim ones in it stayed on our tail. Whoever they were, they were following us.

"They still got us," the driver said.

"I know."

"Where next?"

I leaned forward in the seat. "I'll wager ten dollars you can't lose them," I said.

He grinned happily. "You lose, buddy."

"I'd love to lose."

The grin widened, then disappeared entirely. He had no time for grinning now. He instead devoted himself whole-heartedly to the task of losing our tail. He was a professional and he gave me my money's worth.

He gunned the car north along Madison Avenue, slowed down a little, then shot through 42nd Street on the yellow light. The light was red for the boys behind us. This didn't bother them. They ran the signal, narrowly missed a light pickup truck, and stayed with us.

The cab driver swore softly. He took a corner on two wheels or less, put the pedal to the floor for the length of the block, ran a red light on his own and went the wrong way on a one-way street. Then he ripped around another corner, shot along an alleyway between two warehouses, drove three blocks normally, and let out a long sigh.

"Ten bucks," he said. "Pay the man."

Our tail was gone, if not forgotten. I put a crisp ten dollar bill into his outstretched palm and watched it disappear. I turned to the girl, who was as wide-eyed as ever, if not so frightened. I noticed for the first time that she was quite beautiful, which was fine with me. If one is going to make a practice of rescuing maidens in distress, one might as well select lovely maidens.

"Oh," she said. "Oh, thank you."

I asked her where she wanted to go next. She was flustered. "I really don't know," she said. "I . . . I was so frightened. They were going to kill me."

"Why?"

She looked away. "It's a long story," she said.

"Then suggest a place where you can tell me all about it."

"I don't know where. They have my address so we can't go to my apartment. I—"

The cab was still cruising in traffic and the meter had an impressive total upon it already. I thought quickly. There was a girl I knew rather well named Carole Miranda. She had an apartment on the western edge of Greenwich Village, and she was in Florida for a month or so. Which meant that her apartment was vacant.

I had a key to it. Never mind why.

"Horatio Street," I told the driver. "Number Forty-nine, near the corner of Hudson."

He nodded and headed the car in that direction. I had a few dozen questions to ask the girl but they would all keep until we got to Carole's apartment. In the meanwhile we both sat back and enjoyed the ride. She fell back in her seat in an attitude of total collapse, which was her way of enjoying the ride. I looked at her, which was my way.

35

A beautiful girl. Her hair was short and jet black and it framed a pale oval face. Her skin was cameo white. Her small hands rested in her lap. She had thin fingers. Her nails were not polished.

It was hard to tell much about her figure. Her body was wrapped up in a heavy black cloth coat that left everything to the imagination. My imagination was working overtime.

"We're here," the driver told me.

"We're here," I told her. She opened the door on her side and I followed her out of the cab. The numbers on the meter were high enough for me to give him a five dollar bill and tell him to keep the change.

We stood on the sidewalk in front of a remodelled brownstone with a vaguely cheerful air about it. The windows had windowboxes which held flowering plants in better weather. The building's wooden trim was freshly painted in bright reds and blues. A wreath of holly decorated the blue front door.

"Where are we?"

"A friend's apartment," I told her. "The friend is out of town. You'll be perfectly safe here."

This satisfied her. On the way to the door she held my arm and relaxed a little against me. I opened the front door, unlocked the inner door in the vestibule with one of the keys Carole had given me. We walked through a hallway lit with shaded blue bulbs and up two flights of stairs. The stairs squeaked in protest.

"This is exciting," she said.

"It is?"

"Like an illicit affair," she said. "Where is this place? The top floor?"

I told her it was.

"God," she said. "Then it's not so exciting. Nobody would be able to carry on an illicit affair after a climb like this. Besides, my nose bleeds at heights."

We managed the remaining two staircases. I found the door to Carole's apartment, hoped that she was really out of town, stuck a key in the lock and opened the door. I fumbled for a lightswitch, found it, and brightened the room.

"Now you can tell me all about it," I said.

"I—"

"But first I'll build some drinks. Wait a moment."

She waited a moment while I remembered where Carole kept her liquor supply. I found a bottle of good scotch and a pair of glasses. I put the scotch in the glasses, kept one for myself and gave her the other. We clinked them together ceremoniously and drank.

"My name's Roy Markham," I told her.

She said: "Oh."

"Now it's your turn. But you've got to tell me a great deal more than your name. You've got to tell me who you are and who those men were and why they were chasing you."

"They wanted to kill me."

"Start at the beginning," I said. "And let's have all of it."

She asked for a cigarette and I gave her one, lighted it for her. I took one for myself, then sipped more of the scotch. We sat together in silence on Carole's big blue Victorian sofa for a few moments. Then she started.

"My name is Linda," she said. "Linda Jeffers. I live here in New York. On East End Avenue near Ninety-fourth Street. Do you know where that is?"

I nodded.

"I'm a secretary. Well, just a typist, really. I work at Midtown Life in the typing pool. It's just a job but I like it, sort of."

I waited for her to get to the point. While she was on her way there she told me that she was twenty-four, that she'd come to New York after going to college in southern Illinois, where her family lived, that she wasn't married or engaged or going with anyone, that she lived alone. This was all interesting, but it hardly explained why a pair of thugs wanted to murder her.

"You see?" she said suddenly. "I'm just an ordinary person, really. Just like everybody else."

I could have told her that was not true. She had taken her coat off, and she was wearing a mannish paisley shirt and a black wool skirt, and the body that filled them was not at all like everybody else. It was a superior body.

Her waist was slim, her bust full-blown and good to look at. She had very long legs for a short girl, and when she crossed them I could see that they were as good as they were

37

long, with trim ankles and gently rounded calves. It was a fine body and it went nicely with her fine face.

"Just like everybody else," she repeated oddly. "Except that they want to kill me."

"Who are they?"

"A man named Dautch. I don't know his first name."

"Was he one of the ones following us?"

She nodded. "The shorter one."

"And why is he after you?"

"It's very simple," she said. "I saw him kill a man."

Four

"IT WAS the most horrible thing that ever happened," she told me, her eyes wide and her voice trembling. "I was home at the time. It was three days ago. Monday evening. I live in a building kind of like this one. Except I live in a room, not an apartment. Just a furnished room. It's a nice neighborhood and the rent's cheap enough for me to afford and—"

"You saw a murder," I reminded her.

"Yes. It was at night, around nine. I was in the hallway on the way back to my room. There's no bathroom in my room, I just have this furnished room, and—"

She actually blushed. I didn't know American girls still knew how to accomplish it. I told her to go on.

She did, in a rush. "A man named Mr. Keller had the room at the end of the hallway. His door was open. There were two men in there with Mr. Keller. They were arguing, shouting at each other. I heard Mr. Keller call one of them *Dautch*. That's how I know his name."

"What were they arguing about?"

"I'm not sure. Money, I think. Mr. Keller kept saying he didn't have it and the two men kept on arguing with him. Then the other man—not Dautch—hit Mr. Keller in the stomach. Mr. Keller let out a moan and started to fall forward. Then he straightened up and went straight for Dautch."

"And then?"

She closed her eyes for a second. She opened them and looked at me, her face a mask of fear. "It happened very quickly. I heard a *click*. Then Mr. Keller stepped back with

39

a horrible look on his face. He put his hands to his chest. There was blood coming through the front of his shirt. He started to say something. But before he could say a word he fell over onto the floor."

"What did you do?"

"I'm afraid I must have screamed or something. Because all of a sudden Dautch and the other man were turning and looking at me. Dautch had a bloody knife in one hand. I don't know what would have happened next. But I ran into my room and locked the door. I even pushed the bed in front of it. I was scared they were going to kill me the way they killed Mr. Keller."

"But they left you alone?"

She nodded. "One of them wanted to break down my door and take care of me. That's the way he said it. But the other told him they couldn't waste time. I just stayed where I was and prayed. I was sitting on the edge of the bed to make it harder for them to open the door. Then I heard them going down the stairs. It sounded as though they were dragging something heavy."

"Keller's body?"

She shuddered. "It must have been. I . . . I stayed right where I was for about half an hour. I was scared stiff, too scared to move. Then I moved the bed out of the way and unlocked my door and went back to see if Mr. Keller was still there. I thought I could help him if he was still alive. But I knew he was dead, I was sure of it. Anyway, I thought I could call the police."

"The body was gone."

"That's right," she said. "There . . . there wasn't even any blood on the rug, nothing to show that anything had happened. I even started to think it was my imagination or something. I knew I couldn't call the police. They would tell me I was crazy. I kept reading the newspapers to see if they found Mr. Keller anywhere. But they didn't."

"So you never got in touch with the police," I said. I thought it over. "Well, I can do one thing for you. I can find out if Keller turned up."

"How?"

"By calling the police and asking them. That's simple

40

enough, wouldn't you say? Could you give me a full description of the man?"

She stared at me for a moment or two, then described Keller for me. I went over to the phone and dialed Police Headquarters. I asked for Hanovan at Homicide. He answered the phone gruffly.

"Roy Markham," I told him. "I'm looking for an unidentified corpse, male, around thirty-five, dark brown hair, sallow complexion, going bald in front, about five-eight, medium build. You turn up anything like that since Monday night?"

"Why?"

"I just wondered."

"To hell with you," Hanovan snapped. "Listen—"

"You listen," I said sweetly. "I'm supposed to receive full cooperation from all police officers. Don't you remember? Now give me a little of that cooperation, damn you."

He was silent for a long moment. Then he said he would check. I held the line while he disappeared for a few minutes.

"Nothing," he said finally. "Nothing even close on the unidentified list. Nothing even close on the identified list. You gonna tell me what this is all supposed to be about or should I guess?"

"You may guess," I told him. "And thanks very much for your cooperation."

I hung up and turned to Linda. "Your Mr. Keller hasn't put in an official appearance yet," I said. "So evidently there's little point in your contacting the police."

"How come they told you that?"

"We'll get to that later," I said briskly. "Let's get back to this fellow Dautch. He was after you tonight. Is that the first you've heard of him since the murder?"

"No. He . . . he called me the next day. At least I think it was him. I picked up the phone and a voice told me to forget everything I saw last night or I would get hurt. Dautch rang off before I could say a word." She paused. "I've had a few more calls like that since then. Always the same voice. Sometimes he's been very . . . explicit. About what would happen if I didn't forget Keller. He said filthy things, things he would do to me."

"And then you saw him tonight?"

41

She hesitated. "I ate a late dinner downtown tonight. I had the feeling that somebody was following me but I didn't see anybody. But I didn't want to go home. I went to a movie by myself on Broadway. And even in the theater I felt that there was somebody watching me. It's a terrible feeling. The picture was lousy but I stayed for the whole double feature. I was afraid to go home. And then finally I had to leave."

"And you saw Dautch?"

"That's right. That's how I . . . landed in your lap, I guess. That's what happened, isn't it?"

"Worse things have happened."

She smiled. "You're sweet," she said. "Anyway, I was on Forty-second Street and I saw him, him and the other man. They were behind me and I looked at them and they looked at me. I don't think they were going to try anything. I think they were just following me waiting for a chance to get me alone. I ran for the nearest cab. It happened to be the one you were getting into but I didn't let that stop me." She grinned. "I just hauled open the door and hopped inside. I don't think it was too ladylike but I wasn't worried about it then."

I thought it over. There had to be something I could do for the girl but I was damned if I could put my finger on it. A man was trying to kill her and all she knew was his last name. I could try to find out who he was, could try to discourage him from bothering her any more. I could find out more about Keller and try to solve things completely—by sending Dautch to the chair.

But all that would have to wait until morning.

"Now it's your turn," she said. "Roy, all you did was call the police and they told you everything you wanted to know. Are you a policeman?"

"Not exactly." She looked at me questioningly. "I'm a private detective," I explained.

"That sounds exciting."

"Sometimes," I said.

"What are you working on? Can you help me? Or are you busy? Or do you just do divorce snooping and things like that?"

So I told her about it, because there was nothing much

else to do and because I felt like talking. I ran through my initial discussion with Edgar Taft a night earlier, told her about my pursuit of wild geese in New Hampshire told her about the phone conversation with Taft, the return to New York, the game we were playing with the man in Bedford Hills.

"Then you're not doing anything," she said slowly. "You're just pretending to look for a killer."

"Not exactly."

She looked at me.

"I'm not entirely convinced of this suicide," I said.

"But if the police—"

"The police are occasionally wrong. You've got to consider their position. There's an enormous temptation to write off a homicide as a suicide whenever possible. It makes their work a good bit easier."

"That's terrible!"

I shrugged. "I'm sure they believe it's a suicide," I said. "It certainly follows an established pattern. But I don't think they've investigated as diligently as they might."

"Then you're going to waste your time looking for a killer who doesn't exist?"

"You could call it that." I smiled. "To be truthful, I suspect the suicide verdict is the right and proper one. I suspect my hesitation to accept it stems more from a personal distaste for getting paid for work without performing it. Edgar Taft has hired me. He's paid me a sizeable retainer and will pay me more. I can't abandon the case, much as I'd like to. So I might just as well give value in return, if it's possible."

She was silent. I looked at her and saw how pretty she was. I wondered where Dautch and his friend were, and what they were doing. I wondered why Keller had been murdered.

"Besides," I said, "there are a few points here and there that bother me. People in Cliff's End seemed reluctant to talk to me about Barbara Taft. There was a secret somewhere that no one was saying anything about. God alone knows what it might be. Probably just my imagination. But I want to take a closer look."

"You're not going back up there?"

"Not yet. Not until we straighten out this Dautch-Keller business, anyway. But I'll probably get back there in time. I'd dearly like to delay my trip until the spring, though. It's cold in New Hampshire."

We sat there and finished our drinks. It took me that long to remember what time it was. It was very late.

I stood up.

"Where are you going, Roy?"

"Back to my hotel. It's late. We both need our sleep."

"Don't go, Roy."

"No?"

"No."

"Why not?"

"Because I don't want you to."

Maybe it was too late for me. I was thick-headed, more so than usually. I stood looking at her while she stood up and moved closer to me.

"I don't want to stay here alone," she said.

"Frightened?"

She nodded.

"I suppose I could sleep on the couch," I suggested, idiotically. "I'd be right here then. In case you wanted me for anything."

She laughed, a sweet girlish laugh. She came close to me and was all at once in my arms, her face pressed against my chest. My arms went around her at once and I held her close. I may have been an idiot, but there are limits.

I tilted her face up and found her mouth with my own. I kissed her. Her lips were sweet. Her own arms went around my neck and her soft young body was tight against me.

"You silly man," she was whispering. "You're not going to sleep on the couch. You're going to sleep in the bed, you silly old thing, and so am I. And that way you'll be right there when I need you. And I'll need you."

And then she kissed me again.

We moved softly through the apartment, turning off lights and discarding articles of clothing. We found Carole's bedroom in the darkness, and we found her bed in the darkness, and, finally, we found each other in the darkness.

There were violins and muted trumpets and crashing

44

cymbals and all the other orchestral paraphernalia one reads about in cheap novels. There were her breasts, firm and full and sweet, offering their young freshness to me. There was her soft and wonderful body, and there was her small animal voice at my ear making small animal noises.

Then, afterward, there was sleep.

When I awoke I was the only one in the bed. It was bitterly disappointing. I called her name once or twice, fumbled my way out of the bed and into my clothing. Then I found her note. It was pinned to her pillow, and I should have seen it in the first place.

Roy darling, it read. *A working girl must work. I'm off to the typing pool at Midtown Life. I hope I don't drown in it. I get finished with work at five and I'll come right back here. Please be here when I get here. You have the only key, and I'd feel silly as sin cooling my heels in the hallway.*

By the way, your "friend" who lives here has funny taste in clothes. I borrowed one of her dresses. By the way, I think I'm jealous . . .

There was more, but it was a little too personal to repeat. It was also too personal to leave lying around. I read it, smiled a silly smile, and shredded it. I threw the pieces into the toilet and flushed them away.

My watch told me that it was ten-thirty. I found a small restaurant on Hudson Street which was open. Most restaurants in the Village begin serving breakfast at noon—which, when you stop to think about it, makes a considerable amount of sense. Ten-thirty is altogether too early an hour for a civilized man to be awake. I went into the restaurant and ate orange juice, toast, and coffee. It wasn't much but it appeased the inner man.

It was then time to begin annoying the police.

I went to the Homicide division. My boon companion Hanovan wasn't around but he had left word to the effect that I was an abominable nuisance who had to be tolerated. They tolerated me. Someone brought me a copy of the medical examiner's report on Barbara Taft.

I read it carefully, which was only a waste of time. It said essentially what Hanovan had told me a night ago—death

45

had occurred roughly three to five days ago, death had been caused by drowning, and no supplementary injuries were described. There were contusions here and there upon the body of the corpse but they were interpreted as having been caused while the body was in the water. None were on the head, which seemed to kill the notion that she'd been knocked unconscious before being dumped into the river.

I put the report back and asked to see the criminal records of everybody named Dautch. This jarred them a little. They asked why and I told them it was none of their business, which may have been stretching things a bit. But the orders to humor this British idiot had evidently been firm ones indeed. A uniformed policeman brought me a tray filled with cards. There were fourteen of them in all. Who would have suspected that that many persons named Dautch had criminal records in New York City?

I looked through the cards. Four of the men were obviously out of the picture. They were all over fifty, white-haired and feeble. Five more were currently serving sentences in one prison or another. Of the five who remained, one was nineteen years old, two were tall and blond, one was a Negro. The final "suspect," if you want to call him that, just didn't seem to fit the mold. He was a former bank teller who had been convicted once of minor embezzlement and who was now working as a shoe salesman in Washington Heights. I couldn't picture him as the heavy type who'd been giving Linda such a bad time.

I sighed. I lighted a cigarette and returned the tray of cards to the long-suffering policeman. There seemed to be no additional way to bother him, so I left the station.

There was a public telephone booth on the street corner. I went into it and called my answering service. There had been half a dozen calls since I spoke to them last. I jotted down names and numbers on a slip of paper, thanked the properly honey-voiced girl on the other end of the line, and caught a cab back to the Commodore.

It is hard to say which I needed more, the shower or the shave. I had both and felt human again. I put on clean clothes, went to the phone and began calling the names and numbers on the piece of paper.

Dean Helen MacIlhenny came first. She'd had a round-about report of what had happened and wanted to check it with me. I confirmed what she had heard.

"A terrible thing," she said. "I feared this, of course. It's a dreadful thing when a student ends his or her life."

"You were afraid it would happen?"

"Of course," she said. "Weren't you, Mr. Markham? Neither of us suggested the possibility, of course. One never does. But one always fears suicide when a moody youngster is missing. It's one of the less pleasant facts of life. Or of death."

I agreed that it was unpleasant.

"And it happens once or twice a year," she went on. "Even at a small college like Radbourne. You can count on it—one, two suicides each year. It's awful that it had to happen to someone like Barbara. I thought a great deal of the girl. Difficult to handle but worth the handling."

We talked some more, then ended it. I told her I might be coming up to Cliff's End soon to round out the case. She assured me that I should always be welcome there and that she'd do anything she could to assist me.

I made three more calls, none of them having anything to do with Barbara Taft. One was to a tailor who had a suit ready for a preliminary fitting. I told him I was damnably busy and made an appointment for a week later. My bank had a check of mine that I'd written standing up. The signature was different from normal and they wanted to check with me before honoring it. I told them to go ahead. Another number turned out to belong to a man who wanted to sell me some life insurance. When I found out what he wanted I told him that it was sneaky of him to leave a number with no explanation. Then I told him to go to the devil and rang off on him.

That left two calls to make. One was to a tabloid newspaper. A reporter with gravel in his throat asked me if I had any statement to make in regard to my role in "the Taft case." I told him I'd been retained by Edgar Taft. He asked me what else I had to say. I said that was all and rang off.

Then I called Edgar Taft himself.

47

"Just wanted to check with you," he said. "Got anything yet?"

"Not yet."

"I've been thinking," he said. "Listen, they think she killed herself. They think she drove all the way from New Hampshire to New York just to throw herself into the Hudson. That make any goddamned sense to you?"

"How do you mean?"

"Hell," he said. "Think about it, Roy. Now let's forget about the kind of girl Barb was. I say she wouldn't have killed herself in a million years, but let's forget that for a minute. Suppose she wanted to do it, she was depressed, maybe she was a little sick in the head. Okay?"

"All right. But—"

"Let me finish," he said. "Now, wouldn't she just go ahead and kill herself there in Radbourne? Or maybe race her car and crack it up on the road? Hell, why should she drive all the way into New York, go straight into the city without even stopping at home, then park the car neat as you please and take a jump in the river? It doesn't add up."

"Unless she wanted to see somebody here first."

"You mean some guy?"

"A man or a woman. Anyone."

He didn't say anything for a moment. "Maybe," he said. "I guess it could have been that way. But I can't see it, Roy. I know somebody killed her."

He paused. "You'll really work on it, won't you? That cop sounded so goddamned sure of himself I think he was measuring me for a padded cell of my own. Don't just play along with me, Roy. Don't just humor me. If you don't want to work for me, tell me. I can get somebody else."

"I want to work for you, Edgar." I wasn't lying. There *were* too many loose ends for me to accept the suicide pitch that easily. "I think there's a lot in what you've just said. I don't know what I can accomplish, but I want to work on it."

"That's all I wanted you to say." He laughed mirthlessly. "I'm a pest," he went on. "I'll probably call you once a day. Ignore me, Roy. I'm used to yelling at people until I get results. Just do what you have to do and ignore me."

I wanted to tell him it would be as easy to ignore a

tornado. Instead I repeated that I'd do what I could. Then
I replaced the receiver and left the hotel.

That afternoon was a painful process of calling people and
checking leads that didn't even begin to develop. All I succeeded in obtaining were some negative results. A friend in
the newspaper morgue at the *Times* brought me what copy
had appeared concerning Barbara Taft. There was next to
nothing, and none of it helped.

I ran through other sources and drew other blanks. I
managed, in short, to kill a batch of hours until all at once it
was five o'clock. That made it time to go back to Horatio
Street. I had to be there when Linda arrived. After all, I
didn't want her to cool her heels in the hallway, as she had
put it.

I caught a cab and let my driver worry about the rush hour
traffic. He sweated and cursed his way to Horatio Street. I
got out of his taxi, paid him, tipped him, and went into the
building.

I walked into the vestibule, stuck my key in the door. I
opened it and started inside.

Some sixth sense warned me. It warned me just in time,
and I stepped back quickly.

The sap whistled past my ear.

I caught the hand that held it, twisted quickly and moved
forward. My man spun around. I let go of him and sank a
fist into his middle. He folded up and I hit him in the face.

But there was another one. He had a sap, too, and he hit
me on the head with it. The world spun around and I got a
glimpse or two of celestial bodies. I recognized Mars and
Saturn. And a boatload of miscellaneous stars.

I went down to one knee. The first one—the one I had
belted, the one who had missed me with *his* blackjack—was
standing against one wall, doubled up in pain and looking
unhappy. The other one was ready to hit me over the head
again.

I rolled out of the way. He missed me—evidently neither
of them could do much against a moving target. I picked
myself up and threw myself at him and we both went down
to the floor with me on top. I took one hand and hit him in

the face with it. The room was still rocky and my head hurt horribly, so I took my hand and hit him again.

It was a mistake.

Because, while I was busy lying there and pounding one clown in the face, the other clown had time to make a partial recovery. I remembered him a little too late. I started to get out of the way but this time, by God, he knew how to nail a moving target.

The sap crashed over the back of my head and I flopped onto the floor as a fish flops into the bottom of a boat. The whole bloody galaxy paraded itself in front of my eyes this time. I even saw Uranus.

Then all the stars and planets winked and were gone. The world turned black and grew quiet.

And that was that.

Five

FIRST I heard voices.

The voices were high and soft and gentle, and for an unhappy moment or two I thought I had died and gone to heaven. Then reality returned; no angels possessed such thick accents, such ear-bending overtones of native New York. Angels, of course, speak the Queen's English—or what's a heaven for?

"He must be dead, Bernie," one of the angels was saying. "Lookit the guy. He ain't moving."

"He ain't dead," Bernie said.

"Yeah?"

"Yeah."

"Who says?"

A superior snort from Bernie. "You're a stupid lug, Arnie. You ain't looked at him, you lug. He's breathin'."

"Yeah?"

"Yeah."

Silence for a moment. The one named Bernie seemed to be right. I *was* alive. I could tell because I could feel my head. I didn't really want to but I couldn't help it. It felt as though someone had dropped a pneumatic hammer upon it. I began to remember the pair of clowns who had waited for me, the sap that had put me out of the picture.

"You're full of it, Bernie. He's dead."

"Wanta bet?"

"How much?"

Difficult as it was, I rolled over a bit and opened an eye or two. The light was a shaft of yellow pain that burned straight through my brain. "Hello," I said pleasantly. "Hello, Bernard. Hello, Arnold. You'd better save your money, Arnold. I'm not dead yet. Almost, but not quite."

"Jeez!"

"Precisely," I said. "That's it exactly." I made the mistake of trying to stand up. It didn't seem to work. My legs tried their best but proved unequal to their task. The room rocked and I sat down again. I was still in the hallway of Carole's building on Horatio Street and it was beginning to look as though I'd be there until the end of time.

"Bernard," I said. He stepped forward. I reached into my jacket pocket and found that they'd left me with my wallet. I took it out and found a dollar bill in it. I folded the dollar crisply and passed it to Bernard.

"What's that for, Mister?"

"For being a good boy," I said. "For running to the nearest drugstore and bringing Uncle Roy a triple Bromo Seltzer."

"Who's Uncle Roy?"

"I am," I said. "Now get that Bromo, will you?"

He gave me an uncertain nod. He punched Arnie in the arm and they took off, heading out of the building and down the street. I wondered if I would ever see them again. Probably not, I decided. When you're fool enough to give a twelve year old child a dollar, you shouldn't expect to see him again.

I tried to get up again. This time it worked, even though it felt miserable. I stumbled through the vestibule and sat down outside on the stoop in front of the building with my head in my hand. A passing couple stared at me oddly. I didn't blame them in the least. I shook a cigarette free from the crumpled pack in my pocket and managed to get it lighted. I sucked harsh smoke into my lungs, coughed, then took another drag from the cigarette. The world swam around for a few seconds and came back into focus. My head still ached.

It would probably be doing that for awhile.

I didn't remember Linda until I glanced at my watch. It was six-thirty. I had been unconscious for about an hour, and during that time Linda must have returned from work. I thought about the welcome the pair of thugs must have given her and my stomach started to turn over.

They had her now. And I had a headache and a bad conscience. I wondered where they had taken her, what they had done or were going to do with her.

Dautch had her, of course. But how the hell he managed to pick her up was beyond me. I was fairly certain they hadn't managed to follow us the night before. Our cab driver had been a master, and he had lost them neatly. They could have picked up her trail at her office, of course. If they knew she worked for Midtown Life, they could have watched the building and followed her home.

But they were there before she arrived. Before I arrived, for that matter.

Which meant they must have recognized me. They must have seen me in the cab with Linda, must have known who I was. Then they picked me up at the Commodore during the day and followed me and—

Fine.

But how did the bloody bastards manage to get back to Carole's apartment building before I did?

"Hey, mister—"

I looked up, and my faith in America's youth was restored. Bernie and Arnie stood before me. Bernie was holding out two large paper cups, one filled with water, the other with Bromo powder. I took them from him, poured the water into the Bromo, and watched it fizz the way it does in the television commercials. Then I drank it down, and it tasted horrible.

But it helped. I took a deep breath, dragged once more on my cigarette, and got to my feet.

"Here's your change, mister."

"Oh, no," I said. "That's yours."

"Yeah?"

"A birthday present from your Uncle Roy," I said.

"It ain't our birthday."

"A Christmas present," I said. "Christmas comes soon, you know."

"We know," Arnie said. "Mister, listen. Bernie and me hang

53

around here almost all the time. You ever want a favor, you just ask us. We'll help you out."

I patted them on the head and told them that was fine. I walked away, wondering what possible help two twelve-year-olds could possibly be to me. Perhaps they could fetch me another bromo the next time I walked into a cosh. That was something.

A cab was heading uptown on Hudson Street. I hailed it and sank gratefully into the seat. This time no sweet young brunette tugged open the door and climbed in after me. I rode by myself, and I was lonely.

The hard part was finding a place to begin.

Linda Jeffers was gone, if not forgotten. As far as I could determine, she stood a fairly good chance of getting her brains shot out of her head. I couldn't quite understand Dautch's motives; the girl obviously wasn't going to run for the police, and even if she did he remained pretty much in the clear.

But the fact remained that Dautch and his bully boys were chasing her and had caught her. Maybe she had been feeding me a story—maybe she was running from Dautch for another reason entirely, and no man named Keller had been murdered at all. Whatever had happened, I had to do something. I had to find a girl.

I thought of going to the police. The idea made a certain amount of good sense. There were approximately twenty thousand policemen in the city of New York, and there was only one of me. They could do a better job of manhunting —or womanhunting, as the case may be—than I could, if only by sheer weight of numbers.

But what was I supposed to give them? I had a name— Dautch—and I'd already determined earlier that they couldn't match that name to a record in police files. I had another name—Linda Jeffers—but that wouldn't do them much good either. And I had a farfetched tale of accidentally seen murder which I was beginning to lose faith in on my own.

They would laugh their heads off at me.

I decided to find out a little bit more about Linda Jeffers. She had said that she lived on East End Avenue near 94th

Street. Maybe I could find out something about her where she lived. Maybe, for that matter, she had changed her mind and had gone home from work first.

I bid goodbye to my taxi at the corner of East End and 93rd. There were four residential brownstones on the block between 93rd and 94th, in addition to the headquarters of the Peruvian embassy and a home for unwed mothers. I passed up the embassy and the foaling pen and made inquiries at the four brownstones. None of them had a tenant named Linda Jeffers, nor had any had a male tenant named Keller.

There were a few more buildings that I tried on the next block, between 94th and 95th Streets. Again I got the same answers. No one knew anything about Linda, or about Keller. Out of sheer desperation I tried a few buildings on 94th itself, thinking I'd mixed things up. I had no luck.

Maybe I'd got things all wrong. Maybe she said West End Avenue. Maybe she said 84th Street. Maybe.

And maybe not.

I grabbed another taxi and returned to the Commodore. Someone was playing games with me and I didn't understand it at all. I had been handy and Linda had tossed me a convenient line of patter designed to keep me from getting in the way. For one reason or another she'd been chased by somebody—and there was no reason to assume his name was really Dautch, since everything else had been a lie. My cab was nearby and I was a pleasant host. I'd been lied to, utilized, and paid off in bed.

And that was that.

I didn't like it. I didn't like getting coshed in a hallway by a pair of thugs simply because some girl was playing me for a sucker. I didn't like chasing wild geese all over metropolitan New York.

I didn't like being used.

And the hellish fact remained that the girl was still in trouble. Somehow or other she had managed to louse herself up. Somehow or other Dautch—or whatever in hell his name was—had gotten hold of her again. I didn't know whether he wanted to kill her or what, but after the chase they'd given us last night he obviously wanted her and she just as obviously wanted to stay away from him.

Well, the devil with her. I had more important things to worry about than a girl who was playing me for a bloody fool to begin with. I stopped at the desk at the Commodore and picked up a few scraps of paper, plus a pair of letters. I stuck them into a pocket without bothering to look them over and told the chap behind the desk to send up a boy with a bottle of scotch when he had the chance. Then I rode the elevator to my floor and went to my room. The elevator ride set my poor head spinning again and I stretched out on the bed for a second or two to get my bearings again.

The doorbell woke me ten minutes later. I had dozed off with amazing ease. I got to my feet, opened the door, and signed for a bottle of scotch. I opened it in a hurry and poured a great deal of it into a water tumbler. It helped. It did an even better job than the bromo seltzer which Bernie and Arnie had brought me.

Then I looked at the papers from the desk. The two letters were bills. I wrote checks to cover them and dropped them into the mail chute in the hall. Next I checked the messages.

One was from Edgar Taft. It said that he had remembered I was without a car and thought I might appreciate the use of one. Besides, he went on, he had no further use for Barb's MG and didn't want to have it around. Accordingly it was parked in the Commodore's garage waiting for me to put it to use.

Which was pleasant. If one is going to have a car, one might as well have a good car. And if I was going to make any additional trips to Cliff's End, it would be a great joy to avoid the nefarious combination of busses and trains I'd been forced to take the first time around.

The other scrap turned out to be the bill from the Commodore. It was the end of the week, and there was my bill, and wasn't that nice of them? I scrawled out a check and made a note to drop it off at the desk on my way out.

My glass was empty. I poured more scotch into it, took a small sip, and all at once the silly thing was empty again.

Strange.

Then it was full again.

And then it was empty again.

Strange, I thought. Fool glass must have a hole in it. Scotch disappears the instant it's poured.

Strange.

Then I was stretched out on the bed, too tired and too drunk to bother removing my shoes. My eyes closed themselves and the world crept away on little cat feet, leaving me floating in the middle of the air.

I dreamed about Linda Jeffers and Barbara Taft. I dreamed about getting hit over the head, about racing through dark streets in a fast taxi that turned into an MG. I dreamed ridiculous dreams and I slept the sleep of the just.

Which may or may not have been fitting.

The phone wailed like a V-2 over London. The blitz had been a long while back, but I still felt like diving under the bed and waiting for the All Clear to sound. Instead I picked up the receiver and mumbled a groggy "Hello" into it.

American telephone operators invariably possess metallic voices. This girl sounded like a robot. "Mr. Roy Markham? I have a long distance call for you. Is this Mr. Markham?"

I admitted that it was.

"One moment, please."

I waited the moment, as she had requested. Then a voice came over the line.

"Mr. Markham?"

"Who is this?"

"Helen MacIlhenny," the voice said. "The dean of women at Radbourne."

"Oh," I said. "What is it?"

"I'm sorry to bother you," she said. "Were you sleeping?"

I grunted. I wondered what time it was. My watch was still on my wrist; I hadn't remembered to take it off before passing out. It said 3:48 but I refused to believe it.

"What time is it?"

"Time?" She sounded stupefied. "Time?"

"Time."

"Oh," she said. "A quarter to four. Mr. Markham, something terrible has happened."

57

She didn't have to tell me that. Something perfectly dreadful had happened, by God. Someone had called me in the middle of the bloody night.

"Mr. Markham? Are you there?"

"I'm here."

"I hate to call you at this hour," she went on. "But I just heard, it was just discovered, and I thought you would want to know right away. Because it fits in with what you're doing, of course. It's horrible, but it fits in."

"What does?"

"Do you remember Gwen Davison?"

I remembered a large-breasted girl, a girl who had roomed with Barbara Taft, a girl who hadn't been much help to me.

"Yes," I said. "I remember her. Why?"

She searched for the right words. "She . . . she was found, Mr. Markham."

"I didn't know she was missing."

"No, that's not what I mean. She was found . . . dead. She was murdered."

My face fell.

"Murdered," Helen MacIlhenny went on. "She was stabbed to death on the campus. A pair of students found her. And do you remember a boy named Alan Marsten?"

The beatnik type, the one in Grape Leaves. "I remember him."

"The police are holding him. They've accused him of the murder. They think he killed her."

Things were happening much too quickly for me.

"I thought you might want to know," she went on briskly. "I felt this might . . . fit in . . . with your investigation of Barbara's death. Don't you think?"

"You were right."

"And while it's a bad time to call—"

"I'm glad you called," I told her, honestly enough. "This puts everything in a new light. How long does it take to drive from New York to Cliff's End?"

The question caught her by surprise. "Why . . . five or six hours, I believe. Why?"

"I'm coming right up," I said. "I'll be there as soon as I can. Will you be awake?"

Her voice was grim. "I shall be awake, Mr. Markham. I doubt that I'll get much sleep for the next several days. I couldn't sleep even if I had the time. And I don't have the time."

"Then I'll see you shortly," I said. "And thanks again for the call."

My clothes felt as though I had slept in them, probably because I had. I stripped, took a fast shower, and dressed again. The slight pain of a hangover had taken the place of the thunderous throb that the blackjack had given me. I took a quick nip of scotch from the bottle, a hair of the dog, as it were. Then I went down to the lobby.

"There's a car for me," I told the doorman. "An MG that a man left for me. Will you get it?"

He nodded and ran off to get it. He had it pulled up in front a few moments later, a fire-engine red affair that was sleek and low and lovely.

"Hell of a car," the doorman assured me. "Bet you can really travel in a wagon like that one."

I told him I hoped so. I gave him a dollar and got into the bucket seat behind the wheel. I hadn't driven a sports car in a long while but it all came back quickly enough. I wrapped myself up in the safety belt, got the car going, put it into low and started up.

A gas station attendant filled the small tank and gave me enough road maps to get me to Cliff's End. I studied them for a few minutes, figured out the right route and marked it on the various maps with a pencil. Then I put the maps on the seat beside me and aimed the car at the East Side Drive. That was the fastest way out of the city.

The car was a demon on wheels. Traffic was light at that hour, since not everyone was as much of a fool as I was. I kept the accelerator pedal close to the floor and the car moved along speedily.

I was in Connecticut long before daybreak. There was one long lovely stretch of road that ran right through Connecticut, and the traffic was heavy on that road, but all the cars were heading toward New York—batches of early-morning commuters on the way to Madison Avenue. No one seemed to be heading north and I had the whole road to myself.

The MG sang to me and we moved across Connecticut and into Massachusetts. It was a clear day once it got started with the sun hot and heavy in the sky. There was a slight breeze but nothing strong. There was no snow falling and hardly any left on the roads, which was a blessing.

When the car and I neared the New Hampshire border the weather remained the same but the road conditions were worse. Snow was piled up on the sides of each road I took, and here and there the paved surface was slippery. With a less sure-footed car I would have had to take it easy, but the MG knew how to hold onto the road. The pedal stayed near the floor and the car went on speeding madly.

Gwen Davison was dead. Alan Marsten was supposed to have killed her. And Barbara Taft's suicide was looking a little less like a suicide every minute.

Confusing.

Dean MacIlhenny had guessed it would take five or six hours to get to Cliff's End. I could understand why—it was a hellish trip from the New Hampshire line on, with winding roads and rotten weather. Five or six hours would have been good time.

But Barbara Taft's car was hell on wheels. I made the trip in four hours flat.

Six

I DROVE straight to Helen MacIlhenny's home, a small house on a tree-lined street. The porch light was on and other lights burned in what seemed to be the living room. I left the MG at the curb, walked up a snow-covered path to the door. I rang the bell and she opened the door for me.

"You've gotten here so quickly," she said. "Oh, is that Barbara's car? Or have you one like it?"

"It's Barbara's. Or was. Her father is letting me use it."

"It's quite a car," she said. "I've always wanted to ride in one of those little things. Men used to take me riding, but that was in the rumble seat days, I'm afraid. No more." Her eyes brightened. "But I'm letting you freeze yourself. Come right inside, Mr. Markham."

She poured coffee into cups and we sat sipping it. "I was just ready to go to my office," she said. "I'm due there in half an hour, at nine o'clock. But I thought perhaps I'd go early in case you arrived at an early hour. You got here sooner than I expected."

"It's a fast car."

"It must be. Mr. Markham, this is a terrible situation. It's . . . it's dreadful."

I did not say anything.

"Gwen Davison murdered. Murder is an exceedingly ugly word, Mr. Markham. Bone-chilling."

"Where was she found?"

"In her own room, the room she shared with Barbara. She was killed with a knife, slashed in the stomach and across the breasts and—"

61

She broke off and turned away.

"I think you told me they're holding the Marsten boy," I said. "How did they come to suspect him?"

"It was his knife. One of the students recognized it and the police picked him up. He admitted it was his knife when they showed it to him."

"Did he confess?"

"No."

I lighted a cigarette. "Did he come up with an explanation?"

"He's a strange young man," she said. "His defense is a passive one, Mr. Markham. He has said that someone must have stolen the knife from him. He refuses to say where he was when Gwen was killed. He must have killed her."

"But no one saw him?"

"No."

"When was she killed?"

"Around midnight."

I thought it over. "In her dormitory room?"

"That's right," she said. "Male students are not allowed in the women's dormitories at that hour, needless to say. But I've hardly so much as thought about that." She managed a tiny smile. "It's a relatively minor infraction of the rules. In comparison to murder, that is."

Gwen Davison was dead and Alan Marsten seemed to be her killer. And somewhere there had to be a connection between this new death and the death of Barbara Taft.

Finding it was something else.

"Where's Alan now?"

"In jail," she told me. "The jail in Cliff's End isn't really much of a prison, Mr. Markham. It's just a room in the little police station with a few bars across the door. There's rarely anything resembling a serious crime here. Once in a while a student becomes intoxicated and spends the night in the cell. We've never had a . . . a murder before. Not to my memory, and I've been here a good many years."

I didn't bother mumbling that there was a first time for everything. I put out my cigarette in a small crystal ashtray, finished my coffee and got to my feet. "I'll want to see Marsten," I said. "Do you think you could fix that up for me with the police force?"

She smiled. "It's already arranged. I anticipated your wishes. They're expecting you."

I told her I'd drop her off at her office on the way. She was pleased by this, since it would give her a chance to ride in the MG.

"It's been a long time," she said. "Do I have to fasten this safety belt thing?"

"We won't be going that fast."

"That's good," she said. "It's like an airplane. If any of the students see their good dean breezing along in this little thing I'll never live it down."

I grinned at her. "I'll bet you've had lots of men take you for a spin."

"But then the cars were all Marmons and Stutz Bearcats, Mr. Markham. This is quite different."

I dropped her off at her office. She told me the ride was much better than a Marmon or a Stutz. Then she told me how to find the police station. "It's not much," she explained. "If you don't look closely you won't even see it."

I found out what she meant. A small white frame building, one story high and less than twenty feet wide, crouched at the end of a dead-end street. It was the police station. A uniformed sergeant sat behind an old oak desk. He was the only man in the station house.

I told him who I was and what I wanted.

"Ayeh," he said. "Ayeh." His voice was resolutely New England. "You're the Englishman the dean was talking about. Come for a look at our killer, did you?"

"That's right."

"Hear ye want him for something else. A killing he did in New York."

"Well," I said. "I'm not so sure about that."

"Shouldn't be hard to extradite him," the man said. "Though I reckon we can try him here about as well. You want to see him now, do you?"

"Yes."

"This way."

He led me to the back of the building. There was a heavy wooden door there. Its single window was barred with rusty slabs of iron. I looked between the bars. Alan Marsten was sitting on the edge of an ancient army cot, his head in his hands. He did not look up.

The police officer fitted a key into a lock and turned it. The door swung open, its rusted hinges creaking in metallic protest at this invasion of privacy.

"There he be," the policeman said. "You say what you want with him. I'll pay no mind." He winked a rheumy eye. "I know how you big-city detectives work," he added confidentially. "I'll be aways up in the front there. I won't hear a thing. You knock that killer around a mite, I won't know about it."

I stepped into the cell. The door creaked shut and a key turned in the lock again. I listened to his receding footsteps as he left me alone with the boy.

I said: "Alan."

He looked up, blinked, recognized me. "You," he said. "The private fuzz. What do you want?"

"To talk."

"Yeah," he said. "Talk. Solid. You got any straights? They lifted mine."

"Straights?"

"Cigarettes," he said. "It's slang. You know—the picturesque language the American peasants speak."

I gave him a cigarette, scratched a match and presented him with a light. He took a very deep drag, coughed, blew out a lungful of smoke. "Thanks," he said. "I go nuts without a cigarette every few minutes. I smoke too much, I'll get cancer, I don't care. It's a laugh, huh? I won't live long enough to get cancer. They'll hang me. Or what is it they do in New Hampshire? Hang you or gas you or electrocute you or what?"

I told him I didn't know.

"Maybe they abolished the death penalty. Probably not— you can't expect much from a backwards hole like New Hampshire. And even if they did, then I'd stand trial in New York. You want me for Barb's murder, huh?"

I didn't say anything.

64

"Hell with it," he said. "Barb's dead. They can do whatever they want to do. I don't give a damn."

"Did you kill Gwen Davison?"

He looked at me, surprised. "Now that's a fresh angle," he said. "Everybody else asks why I killed her. They don't even think I might be innocent. You're a breath of fresh air, man."

"Did you?"

He looked away again. "No," he said. "I didn't. Do you believe me?"

"I don't know."

"Well, that something," he said. "That's the closest yet. At least you didn't come right out and say no, man. You're way in front of second place."

"She was killed at midnight," I said.

"I'm hip."

"Where were you at the time?"

He shrugged.

"Where were you, Marsten? Listen, you bloody fool—you're neck deep in this affair, whether you know it or not. The cop at the desk gave me permission to beat the truth out of you if I feel like it. He says he doesn't much care whether you hang in New Hampshire or New York. Why don't you try talking?"

His eyes were defiant. "I was all alone," he said. "How's that for an alibi? I was all alone and nobody saw me. I wandered around, here and there. That all right?"

"You're lying."

Another shrug. The little fool didn't seem to give a damn whether I believed him or not.

"How did your knife wind up in Gwen's body?"

"I don't know."

"Someone take it from you? And what were you doing with a knife in the first place?"

He looked thoroughly bored. "Maybe someone took it," he said. "Maybe it grew wings and flew away. I keep it in a drawer in my room. I never missed it until they told me it was used to kill Gwen. Hell, they didn't even tell me. They stuck a bloody knife in front of me and asked me if I saw it before. So I told them. What the hell, they woulda found out anyway."

"And why did you have the knife?"

"I used it to cut my fingernails."

I didn't want to hit him. I knew that the insolence came from fear, that the withdrawal and generally obnoxiousness of his personality was more a defense mechanism than anything else. But a little knocking around wouldn't hurt him. If he was innocent, it might jar him out of his reveries. If he was the killer, then I felt he had it coming.

I said: "Get up."

"Why, man?"

He didn't move. I bunched a hand in his shirt front and dragged him to his feet. I slapped him across the face, hard, and held him with the other hand. He looked startled.

I closed my hand into a fist and hit him in the stomach. I let go of him and he sat down heavily on the bed. His eyes were angry.

"So you're a big man," he said. "Congratulations."

"You want more?"

"No," he said.

"Then you're ready to talk?"

"Yeah," he said. "Sure."

I said: "Barbara Taft was mixed up in something that got her killed. Gwen Davison was in the same thing, in one way or the other. And you're tied in. All I want to know is what it's all about."

He looked at me.

"Well?"

"Oh, to hell with it," he said. "Everybody wants to give it to me in the neck. I thought you were going to be different but you had to come on like a heavy. Edward G. Robinson with an English accent yet."

I didn't say anything.

"You don't get anything from me, man. You're just another bastard like the rest of them. You want to hit me, go ahead and hit me. Maybe it'll make you feel like a big man. Take out all your aggressions."

"I'm not going to hit you."

"No?"

"No."

"Solid," he said. Then get lost, huh? You're a bigger drag than Gwen was."

"Is that why you killed her?"

He frowned. "Jesus Christ," he said. "Here we go again. That was one straight out of television. Why don't you hire a decent writer?"

"I'd like to, but this is a low-budget show. You're not too popular around Cliff's End, Marsten. You might need a friend. If you decide you do, you might call me. The chap on duty will get in touch with me."

"Sure. But don't hold your breath."

I took out my pack of cigarettes, lighted one for myself, then tossed him the pack and a book of matches. "You might want these," I said.

He looked at me, eyebrows raised, for a second or two. I saw wheels turning in his mind. Then he shrugged and stuffed the pack into a pocket.

I went to the door and called for the jailer to come let me out of the cage. Prisons do not exactly have an uplifting effect upon my spirit. I wanted to walk outside and breathe fresh air again. This was a one room small town jail, if you could call it a jail at all. But the air was the air of all prisons everywhere and I didn't care for it.

"Man—"

I turned around. Alan Marsten had a thoughtful expression on his face.

"My old man is rich," he said. "He'll send up one of his expensive lawyers. One of those city cats who can make these hicks look like idiots. He'll get me off, won't he?"

I listened to the measured steps of the jailer. He was not setting any speed records.

"Won't he, man?"

"Maybe," I told him. "It may be interesting to see whether he can or not. Whether they hang you or not."

The jailer opened the door and gave me another conspiratorial wink. He slapped me on the back and I had a strange urge to wipe myself off. I left Alan Marsten wondering whether or not he was going to hang, left the jailer hawking and spitting into a green metal wastebasket at the side of his desk, left the grayness of the police station for the blinding whiteness of sunlight reflected from the snow. The MG was waiting where I had left it, a low-slung kitten with blood-red fur. I drove away very fast.

Mrs. Grace Lipton lived in a large old house on Phillips Street. She rented out rooms to tourists and to a few students who had somehow arranged for permission to live off-campus. Helen MacIlhenny had recommended the boarding house on my first visit to Cliff's End. Now it looked as though I was actually going to have to remain in the town overnight. I paid the old woman three dollars for a night's lodging, lugged my overnight case in from the MG, and took a quick shower.

Dean MacIlhenny was in conference somewhere when I returned to the Radbourne Administration Building. I waited in her office and killed time by putting through a call to Hanovan in New York. I made the call collect, just to see what would happen, and he surprised me by accepting the charges.

"I'm a son of a bitch," he said, with surprising accuracy. "You're actually working on the case."

"Of course."

"Find anything?"

"Enough to cast doubt on your suicide verdict," I told him.

"Yeah?"

I gave him a quick run-through on what had happened at Radbourne, explaining that Barbara Taft's roommate had been murdered by her erstwhile companion, according to the police. He digested this in silence.

Then, "You think he did it?"

"No."

"Any reason?"

"Just a feeling."

I could almost hear him shrugging. "Hick cops," he said. "I figure you know more about it than they do. This is okay, Markham. This is good."

"It is?"

"Yeah. For us, anyway. Look, the Taft kid was mixed up in something, right? We gotta figure it that way. It's no coincidence—whether she knocked herself off or whether

68

she had help, there's still a tie-in between her and the killing up where you are. Right?"

"It would seem that way."

He ignored the sarcasm. "Which ties it to the college," he went on. "It's not a New York case any more. We can't do a thing with it except cooperate with New Hampshire."

I wanted to compliment him on his fearless and tireless dedication to duty. I saved myself the trouble. "Speaking of cooperation," I said.

"Yeah?"

"I can use some assistance," I said. "I had a run-in with a young woman a day or so ago. She gave me a story about witnessing a murder and being in trouble. The name she palmed off on me was a false one and I think her story was just as false as her name. But she's in trouble."

"How do you know?"

"There were a pair of thugs after her. They followed us but we got clear of them. Then the next morning I was waiting to meet her and they were waiting for me."

Hanovan snorted. "You got cold-decked?" The amusement danced through his words.

"There were thirty of them," I said. "And they all had atomic ray guns. I think they made off with the girl and I think they may have killed her."

"Gimme a description."

I gave him a very full description. I even told him she had an appendectomy scare, plus a mole high on the inside of her right thigh.

He whistled happily. "Just a casual acquaintance," he said.

"That's right."

"You got a good life," he said. "This got anything to do with the Taft run-around?"

"No," I said. "It's just a favor you're going to do me. Let me know if she turns up anywhere, or if you get a line on the name Linda Jeffers."

I gave him Dean MacIlhenny's number, plus the number of Grace Lipton's phone. Then I rang off and lighted a cigarette.

Another conversation with Helen MacIlhenny gave me no more in the way of pertinent information. It yielded two things only—a renewed appreciation for the woman, and permission to go through Gwen Davison's room. According to her, the police of Cliff's End hadn't gotten around to searching the room. Evidently the concept of discovering a motive for the murder was out of their ken. Hanovan may have been wrong about a good many things, but I couldn't argue with his opinion of small-town police.

The room in Lockesley Hall was silent and cheerless. The neatness and precision of the dead girl still characterized the room. Everything was clean and in its place, and this made the bloodstained floor just that much more incongruous.

I closed my eyes and saw her standing there, saw a faceless assailant moving toward her with a knife. I wondered why no one had heard her scream, or at least heard the sounds of a scuffle. No girl, however precise and orderly, stands stock-still and permits herself to be stabbed to death.

I guess that she knew her killer. Whoever he or she may have been, Gwen had admitted the killer to her room, had permitted the killer to get close enough to her to stick a knife into her before she could shout for help.

It was something to think about.

So, for that matter, was the idea of a man or boy entering a dormitory at midnight and leaving it after midnight without being seen.

I lighted a cigarette and started to look through her desk. I found piles of school notes from all the years she had been in Radbourne, all classified by subject matter and secured with paper fasteners. Her penmanship was perfect Palmer method, her typing painfully flawless.

All her clothes were folded neatly in the drawers of her dresser. I went through them more as a matter of form than because I expected to find anything. She had a great many sweaters; I guessed she must have been proud of the way she filled them.

Now all she would ever fill was a shroud. And a hole in the earth somewhere.

Something kept me in the room even after I had decided that I was wasting my time, even when I began to feel ghoulish about going through stacks of clothing which she would never wear again. Something kept me hunting methodically for a scrap of a clue, a gram of evidence pointing in one direction or another.

Perhaps it was the total lack of motive for her murder. As even an oaf like Hanovan had been acute enough to realize, there was an obvious connection between Barbara Taft and Gwen Davison. They had lived together and they had died almost simultaneously. Which meant that Gwen's killing had a motive, a reason.

Which I could not seem to locate.

So I went on with my silly search. Maybe it was my detective's sense of smell that kept me going, maybe some sixth sense, maybe some form of intuition.

Whatever it may have been, it was valuable.

It worked.

It worked, as it happened, on the top shelf of Gwen Davison's closet. It worked when I hauled down a hatbox, its sides securely sealed with masking tape. I wondered momentarily why anyone would take the trouble to fasten a hatbox with masking tape. Then I stripped off the tape and had a look.

There was a single manilla envelope in the box. It was eight inches wide by ten inches long and it was fastened by a metal clasp. The clasp looked as though it had been opened and closed many times.

I opened it.

I took out a sheaf of photographs. They were all glossy prints, all just slightly smaller than the dimensions of the manilla envelope which had contained them.

I looked at them.

To be honest, I stared at them. I stared hard at each in turn, and there were six all told. They were not the best existing examples of the art of photography. In some the backgrounds were out of focus. In others the shots were slightly under-exposed.

This did not lessen my interest.

They were the sort of pictures which may be purchased in back rooms of small stores in Soho, or around the Times Square area, or in the tenderloin district of almost any large city. In each picture there was a man and a girl on a bed. In each picture the man and girl were participating in one or another form of sexual intercourse.

Pornographic photographs.

Which in itself was not all that remarkable. Gwen Davison would not have been the first college girl with an interest in vicarious sexual excitement.

But there was more. The faces of the men, in all six photographs, were either turned from the camera or deliberately blocked out from sight. The faces of the girls were plainly visible in each picture. The faces, in two instances, were familiar.

I took one photograph and studied it. The girl in the picture was tall and blonde. She was engaging in sexual relations with a man in a rather bizarre manner and her expression indicated considerable pleasure.

I put the picture away hastily. There is something extraordinarily revolting in the notion of looking at pornographic pictures of a corpse. And this girl was a corpse now.

It was Barbara Taft.

And then I looked once more at the other picture I had recognized. I saw the bright eyes, the full breasts, the pretty face. I saw the dark hair, the trim waist.

I saw the appendectomy scar. I saw—just faintly visible, but unmistakably present—the mole high on the inside of her right thigh.

I saw the face. The face of a girl I had known before, but under a name which was probably false.

Linda Jeffers.

Seven

By THE time I returned to the police station, a younger man had replaced the older one behind the desk. He was tall enough to make me feel short and young enough to make me feel old. He had a forest ranger's build and a boy scout's face. His eyes were blue and very frank.

"Roy Markham," I said. "I'd like to see the Marsten boy."

He motioned for me to sit down. "Pete told me about you," he said. "I'm Bill Piersall. The kid's lawyer is in with him now. Have a seat."

I had a seat. "He's got an honest-to-God Philadelphia lawyer in there," Piersall said. "The Marstens live in Philadelphia. Main Line family. So the lawyer's a Philadelphia lawyer. Isn't that one for the books?"

"It certainly is," I said, to make him happy. It seemed to make him happy at that. "What time did he get here?"

"The lawyer?"

I nodded.

"About an hour ago. Been with him all this time. Wonder what he's got to talk about."

"Did you hear any of it?"

He shook his yellow-topped head. "Not a word," he said. "Well, I did hear a word at that. More than a word. That lawyer said a few things before I left the cell. But I'm damned if he used a word of less than four syllables. Every other one out of his mouth was a regular jawbreaker."

"Have you any idea how long they'll be?"

"No idea," he said. "I guess we just wait for 'em."

We waited for them. It would have been easier to take the

73

picture to Helen MacIlhenny for identification, but I couldn't quite see myself showing pornographic pictures to the Dean of Women. Some men may be able to carry off a play like that. I would have had trouble.

I reasoned that Alan Marsten would be able to tell me who Linda Jeffers was as well as Mrs. MacIlhenny. And there was more to it than that. Unless I was a good distance from the trail, Marsten knew a lot more than he was telling me. The picture might be a chink in his conversational armor, so to speak. Once I put that single card on the table, he might be willing to come out of his shell.

At least it was a possibility. But first of all I had to identify the girl. I'd made a big mistake in telling Hanovan of New York Homicide that my little pigeon with the mole on her thigh didn't have anything to do with Barbara Taft. She was in it up to the top of her pretty head. She and Barbara were part of a bloody set, for that matter—a set of dirty pictures in a straight-laced girl's closet.

Which was interesting.

Things were taking their own sort of shape now, and some of the pieces of a giant jigsaw puzzle were starting to wind up on the table. But I still had far too few pieces to put them together and come up with anything vaguely resembling reality. I needed more, and I hoped Alan could give me some of it.

Right now it looked like blackmail, of course. But it was a blackmail game with six girls caught in the middle, not just one or two. It seemed to have the dimension of a full-scale blackmail ring with a lot of planning back of it and a great deal of potential profits in the offing.

It looked like a great many things. But I was still up six different trees at once. I couldn't begin to know who was doing the blackmailing, much less guess who had done the killing.

I was half finished with a third cigarette by the time Marsten's lawyer put in an appearance. He called commandingly from the cell and Piersall and I walked there. Piersall opened the door and the lawyer stepped out. He was tall and sandy, his bearing stiffly erect, his eyes sharp.

I begged his pardon and stepped past him into the cell.

74

"And who are you, sir?"

"I'm Roy Markham," I said. "I'm going to have a word with your client, counsellor."

He didn't like that at all. He didn't like the idea of my talking with Alan in private, and I didn't want him around when I started showing dirty pictures. Alan settled the argument simply enough by telling the fellow to get lost. He didn't like it one bit, but he got lost.

Piersall locked us up in the cell again.

"So that's your lawyer."

"That's my lawyer," he said. "He's not much to look at, is he? But he's sharp as blue blades. He's a whip. Nothing but the best for Mr. Marsten's boy Alan."

He was still sitting on the edge of his cot. He was smoking one of the cigarettes I had left with him. He didn't sound as happy as his words indicated. He looked even worse—there were worried lines in his forehead and around the corners of his mouth, and I could see nothing but tension in his eyes.

I didn't waste time. I took the picture with Linda in it from the manilla envelope, glanced at it myself, then passed it to him. I asked him if he knew the girl.

He didn't have to answer; his eyes did that for him. There was instant recognition combined with a great amount of shock. His jaw fell and he gaped at me like a goldfish in a bowl.

"There are more pictures in the envelope," I said.

He nodded dully.

"And you've got a few things to tell me," I went on. "This time you're going to talk. You know a bloody bit more than you've said so far and I want to hear it."

He nodded again. "Yeah," he said. "Solid. Where'd you get these?"

"What do you care?"

"Hell," he said. He looked at the picture, then gave it back to me. "I can talk to you now," he said. "You got the picture of Barb, huh?"

"In the envelope."

"That's what I was afraid of. I didn't want to open up about . . . things . . . unless somebody already knew about

75

the pics. I don't know. Silly, I guess. I figured if Barb was dead the pictures at least could stay a secret. You know what I'm talking about?"

"No."

"Oh. What do you know, man?"

I said: "I can guess. Someone took pornographic photographs of six girls, maybe more. Barbara was one of them. She was being blackmailed, being taken for heavy money."

"Right so far."

"That's as far as I've taken it," I said. "Now it's your turn."

He dropped his cigarette to the floor of the cell, covered it with a foot and ground it out slowly and deliberately. He looked up at me finally.

"What do you want to know?"

"You could start with the girl in the picture. Who is she?"

"Name's Jill Lincoln. She was sort of a friend of Barb's. Part of the same crowd."

"Did you know she was being blackmailed?"

He shook his head. "I only knew about Barb. And I didn't know all of it. Only what she told me."

"Go on."

"A couple weeks ago," he said. "I was with her and she was so nervous I thought she was going to turn green any minute. She kept losing track of the conversation, kept wandering off and getting lost in her own words. I asked her what was the matter, what was bugging her."

"And?"

"She wouldn't say. She kept saying everything was all right, she was just worried about an exam she had, some jazz like that. I could tell it was something else. She didn't worry like that about her classes. She just didn't care that much. So I kept hitting her with questions, telling her she should tell me all about it."

He looked away. "We were very close," he said. "Not that I knew everything on her mind, nothing like that. She had her life and I had mine, you know. We weren't even going together as a steady thing. But we were close. We could talk to each other. She had something bugging her, she generally would tell me about it."

76

"Go on."

He shrugged. "So she told me. We were sitting in her car and she flipped open the glove compartment and took out a picture. She handed it to me. It was like the one you showed me. Except with Barb in it. Barb and some cat."

"She showed it to you?"

"Yeah. I almost folded. She didn't even blush or anything, just handed it to me and said 'Here—isn't this cute?' I asked her where the hell it came from."

"What did she say?"

"She didn't exactly say," he told me. "She said somebody was blackmailing her, threatening to send the picture around if she didn't play ball."

I said: "Why should that worry her so much? She's supposed to have run with a fairly fast crowd. Her parents knew that. I'm sure they didn't suspect she was a virgin."

He looked at me. "Use your head, man. There's a difference between knowing your daughter sleeps around a little and seeing a picture of it. And the bastard was going to do more than send a print to Barb's old man. A few prints were going to some school officials. Other prints were going to other people. And then the negative was going to be sold to one of those outfits that sells pictures like that around the country. You know—cut-rate kicks for kiddies. They'd be selling Barb's picture at every high school in America. Get the picture?"

I got the picture. It was an ugly one.

"It meant getting kicked out of school," Alan Marsten went on. "It meant a rotten reputation for a hell of a long time. It meant trouble in spades. Barb didn't like the idea."

"Did she say when the picture was taken?"

"She told me a little of it. There was this party—her and some of her friends and a batch of people from out of the college. Some of the dead-end kids around town, I figure. She got stoned, said she thinks there was something in the drinks besides alcohol. After that she didn't remember. Maybe she didn't want to remember. I don't know."

"And she didn't say who the blackmailer was?"

"Not a word. She wouldn't tell me how much he wanted from her, either. I figured if it was such a big bite I could

77

help her out with it, get some extra dough from my old man. But she didn't want to talk. So we didn't talk."

"And that was all?"

"That was all." He fished in his pocket for cigarettes, selected one. It was bent. He straightened it out with his fingers, put it between his lips. scratched a match and lighted it. He took a deep drag of smoke and blew a cloud of it at the ceiling.

"Then Barb cut out," he said. "I figured she couldn't take it any more, wanted to run away some place and try starting over. Maybe she figured if she left town she could call the bastard's bluff, wait him out or something."

"Then she died."

"Yeah," he said heavily. "You came up here looking for her, came on to me at Grape Leaves with a hatful of questions. I told you to get lost. I figured the way I said. Then I heard she was dead and a whole lot of things didn't matter any more."

"And now you're in jail."

He laughed. "Solid—I'm in jail. And you're asking all the questions and I'm coming through with all the answers. You mind a question, man?"

I told him to go ahead.

"Where'd you find the pictures?"

"In Gwen Davison's closet."

His jaw fell again and his eyes bulged. "You kidding?"

"No."

"I don't get it," he said. "She was the blackmailer? And one of the other girls killed her?"

"Do you think so?"

"What else, man?"

I drew a breath. "She didn't have the negatives," I said. "Just a set of prints."

"Maybe she kept the negatives somewhere safe."

"There's more," I told him. "I can hardly picture a girl like her engineering something like this. It's too complex. There are too many sides to it."

I didn't bother adding that whoever had set everything up obviously had connections with New York—hoods to hire, strings to pull. It was none of his business. It was purely a private headache of mine.

He said: "I guess I don't get it."

"Neither do I. You didn't kill Gwen, did you?"

"Why would I?"

"Maybe you discovered she was in on the blackmail circuit," I suggested. "You were in love with Barbara. You blamed Gwen for Barbara's death. So you murdered her with your knife."

"You don't believe that, do you?"

I didn't. He'd been too surprised by the picture, too surprised that I'd found it in Gwen's room. But it was something to toss at him, whether I believed it myself or not.

"It keeps coming back to the damn knife," he said. "You know what happened with that knife? Hell, you won't believe it."

"Try it out."

"I gave it to Barb," he said. "A few days before I left, I gave it to her. She asked to borrow it. God knows what she wanted it for. I didn't ask. I let her take it." He managed a grin. "Now, who in hell would believe a story like that?"

"I might."

"Yeah?"

"But I don't know if a jury would," I said.

After I left him I found a telephone and put in a call to Jill Lincoln's dormitory. A girl answered the phone almost at once and told me she'd check to determine whether or not Jill was in her room. She checked and determined that she wasn't. I told her there was no message and put the receiver back on the hook where it belonged.

Then I went down the street to the tavern. The next step was to get hold of Jill Lincoln, preferably by the throat. I had a good many questions to ask her and she was going to supply the answers if I had to hold her upside down and shake them out of her. But she would keep—I couldn't find her at the moment, and it was late enough in the day for my stomach to be growling bearishly. Lunch had somehow been left out of the picture that day. Breakfast had been ages ago.

I was starving.

I remembered the small steak and decided it was too small. I told the waiter to bring me the biggest sirloin they could find in the kitchen, with the biggest baked Idaho beside it. In the meanwhile, I added, he should try to find me a mug or two of ale. He brought the ale in a hurry and it went down easily.

Jill Lincoln.

She was quite a girl, I decided. She had switched her initials aound, provided herself with a fresh name, concocted a far-fetched story and made me believe it. She set me up for a rap on the head, then disappeared neatly and left me to chase around the city trying to rescue her.

But why?

It made no more sense than anything else. And no less— because nothing at all seemed to make sense. The most alarming single fact about the entire affair was that the more I learned, the less logical everything became. I kept getting more and more pieces of the jigsaw puzzle, and none of them fit with any of the others. It was incredible.

According to Alan, the blackmail routine was an explanation for Barbara's suicide. I couldn't see it that way myself. She had a great deal of money at her disposal and her father was more than generous. She'd drawn over a thousand dollars before she left Radbourne. So the blackmailer, whoever he was, could hardly have had her with her back to the wall.

So why should she kill herself?

And, further, why run to New York to do it? That still didn't add up. If she were going to commit suicide, she still might as well have done it in New Hampshire.

Which brought it around to murder again. But why would a blackmailer murder a victim? There are simpler ways than that to grow rich. It would be the classic example of killing the goose that lays golden eggs.

The waiter saved me by bringing my steak. I pushed Barbara and Gwen and Jill from my mind forcibly, picked up knife and fork and attacked a hunk of thick red meat. I had two more ales to wash it down and left the table, finally, feeling several pounds heavier and several degrees more at peace with the world. I used the telephone on the wall in the tavern to try Jill Lincoln again. A different female voice answered this time, but the information was the same. Jill was out. I passed up another opportunity to leave a message, returned to my table and paid my check. I went outside and took a deep breath of cold air.

What next? I could run around like a headless chicken if I wanted, but I couldn't see how that would do me much good. Jill was the person I had to see. Until I saw her I was too much in the dark to get anywhere.

The thought crossed my mind that something could have happened to her, that maybe she was in danger in New York. That seemed unlikely, but in this case everything that was unlikely was as apt to happen as everything else. Or maybe she was still in New York—it seemed as though students could be absent from Radbourne for an incredible length of time before anybody noticed or reported their absence.

I gave up, got into Barbara's MG and drove back to Mrs. Lipton's home for wayward detectives. I would have to assume that Jill was somewhere around, that eventually she would go to her dormitory and I could contact her there. In the meanwhile I could sit in a comfortable room, shave the stubble from my face and otherwise take things easy.

I found my way back to the old house and parked in front of it. I killed the engine and pocketed the key. I was halfway to the door before I heard my name called in an urgent whisper.

I turned and saw her.

"Roy," she said. "Come here."

She was by a clump of bushes at the side of the house. I walked to her, not sure whether I was supposed to chuckle appreciatively or to belt the bloody life out of her.

"Hello, Jill."

"Oh," she said. "You found out my name."

"Uh-huh. I saw your picture."

"Roy, I've got to talk to you."

"That's the understatement of the century," I said. "You've got a great deal of talking to do."

"Not here," she said. "Oh, Christ. It's not safe here. Look, can we go to your room?"

"My room?"

"Upstairs," she said.

81

"That's crazy. I'm relatively certain Mrs. Lipton would object to my entertaining college girls in my room. And—"

"Roy."

I looked at her. She knew how to fake fear—I remembered her magnificent act in the taxi when we first met. But I couldn't believe she was faking now. There were beads of perspiration on her upper lip and she had developed a nervous tic under her left eye. Even Actors Studio has trouble teaching one tricks of that order.

"I took a chance coming here, Roy."

"You take a good many chances."

"This was a big one. Let's go to your room. If they see us together they'll kill me."

"If we go to my room, do I get hit over the head again?"

She bit her lip. "I'm sorry about that. Honest, I'm sorry. I didn't know that was going to happen. I'm sorry about a lot of things." She frowned. "Can't we go to your room?"

"Oh, hell," I said. "Sure, we can go to my room. Come on."

Eight

THE SIMPLE course seemed by all odds the best one to pursue. I did not attempt to spirit Jill into Mrs. Lipton's house via a rear window, or send her scuttling up a ladder, or otherwise get her to my room by stealthy methods. No doubt Grace Lipton was already familiar with such methods, since student boarders rented her rooms. Nonchalance appeared a better gambit. I took Jill by the hand and led her through the doorway, into the house, down the hall, past the living room where Mrs. Lipton sat immersing herself in television, up a flight of stairs and into my room. Nobody questioned us, looked askance at us, or otherwise interfered with us.

I closed the door, turned the latch. She tossed her coat over a straight-backed chair while I hung mine on a hook in the small closet. Then she sat down on the bed while I stood lighting a cigarette and watching her through the smoke. She stared back at me in silence while I shook out the match and found an ashtray to drop it into. The fear was still present in her eyes.

"This had better be good," I said.

"It will be."

"And it had better be true. You're quite an effective little liar, Jill."

"You believed all of it?"

"I even went looking for you on East End Avenue. If that's any satisfaction to you."

Evidently it was. A smile turned up the corners of her mouth, then died there as her face took on a serious cast once more. "I'm awfully sorry about that, Roy. I didn't want

83

to feed you a story like that. I kept wanting to break down and tell you the truth. But I couldn't."

"Start at the beginning."

She sighed. "Could I have a cigarette? Thanks. You said something about seeing a picture of me before. When we were out in the cold, I mean. Did you see it?"

I nodded.

"There were six of us, Roy. Me and five other girls. Barb Taft was one of us and—"

"I saw the whole set."

"The six?"

"Yes."

She dragged on the cigarette. "Well," she said. "Well, it's quite a display of artistic photography, isn't it? You probably can figure out most of it, then. We were at a party, Roy. A party in Fort McNair—that's the next town along Route Sixty-eight and it's even smaller and duller than Cliff's End."

"Whose party was it?"

"Some guys in Cliff's End. One of the girls—I think it was Barb but I'm not sure—managed to get herself picked up by one of the guys. His name is Hank, Hank Sutton. He's the leader."

"Of the blackmail mob?"

"That's right, Roy. He's a . . . a gangster. I didn't think they had gangsters in little hick towns like this one. But he's in charge of numbers and bookmaking and God-knows-what-else in this half of New Hampshire. Even when I found out about him, I thought he must be small-time. But he has connections with New York gangsters. I found that out."

I put out my cigarette. "Let's return to the party."

"Sure. Well, it was . . . quite a party. The six of us aren't a bunch of vestal virgins. I guess you figured that out for yourself, didn't you? Well, we're not. But we didn't think it would be that kind of a party. I mean, we figured on some heavy necking, and maybe going the limit if we felt like it."

"You didn't feel like it?"

"We didn't have any choice. I don't know what that bastard Hank put in the drinks, but it worked. God, did it work! I remember the way the party started but that's about

84

all I remember. The rest is a big blank. Then I remember coming out of the fog when they let us out of their cars back on campus. We sat around for two hours drinking coffee and trying to wake up and trying to figure out what happened." She paused dramatically. "Well, in a few days we found out."

I said: "They showed you the pictures?"

She shook her head. "They mailed 'em to us. Each of us got a set of prints in the mail, six pretty little prints in a manilla envelope. No note, no letter, nothing. You can imagine what it was like opening the envelope."

"I know what it was like." I decided to toss her a curve. "I found one of those envelopes. It was in Gwen Davison's closet."

I waited for a monumental reaction. Jill disappointed me. She didn't bat so much as an eyelash, just nodded as if that was perfectly natural.

"Must have been Barb's set," she said. "Don't . . . uh . . . lose them, will you? I wouldn't want them floating around campus. It might be a little embarrassing."

"It might," I agreed. "Let's get back to the pictures. Did this Hank Sutton get in touch with you?"

"On the phone. He told me what he was going to do with the pictures if I didn't 'play ball.' I asked him what playing ball meant. It meant two hundred dollars from each of us. That was a starter. He wanted more money again not too long ago. Just a day or two before Barb disappeared, as a matter of fact."

"How did you pay him?"

"I got together with the rest of the girls. We decided that we had to pay off, at least for the time being. Until we figured out something we could do. Each of us kicked in the two hundred bucks and I carried the loot to Hank."

"You were the messenger?"

She nodded soberly. "Little old me. It was bad enough paying him a cool twelve hundred dollars. That wasn't enough. He decided he liked me. He . . . he made me stay there with him. It wasn't very much fun, Roy."

I could imagine. I looked at her, still nervous but beginning to pull herself together. I was getting plenty of pictures now, including the pornographic ones in the manilla

85

envelope, but outside of that we weren't getting anywhere in particular. I still hadn't the vaguest notion whether Barbara had killed herself or whether she had had help. I still didn't know who had slashed the young life out of Gwen Davison.

I said: "How come you picked me up?"

"In New York? That was on orders, Roy. Orders from Hank Sutton."

"Tell me about it."

She nodded. "Well, Barb took off. You know about that. I thought she was going for money or something, or just trying to run fast and hard to stay away from Hank and Radbourne and the whole rotten mess.

"But instead she killed herself. Hank learned about it almost as soon as the police fished her out of the Hudson. Then he heard you were on the case—I don't know how. So he sent me to New York to work on you."

She paused and narrowed her eyes. "I didn't have any choice, Roy. He told me to go and I went. I was blackmailed into it—he still had the pictures, and as long as he had them I had to do whatever he wanted."

"Go on."

"I went to New York. Hank had men there checking on you. They must have followed you all over the place. I'm surprised you didn't notice them."

"I wasn't looking for them."

"I guess not. Of course, you couldn't know anybody would want to follow you, could you?"

I agreed that I couldn't. She finished her cigarette and managed a smile. It wasn't a very firm one. "So that was that, Roy. I picked you up coming out of the restaurant on Times Square. I ran for your cab and hopped into it. Then those two men—they were some of Hank's New York friends —pretended to be chasing me. They weren't supposed to chase too hard. Even with an ordinary cabby we would have gotten away. The driver we had lost them so nicely it didn't look like a set-up at all."

"That's true enough. What were you supposed to do next?"

"Just what I did—give you a phony story, find out what you knew about Barb and whether or not you were going to invesigate. Hank figured that if you stayed on the case you'd find out about the pictures, and it would be messy. He thought I could find out whether you were interested in it or if you were going to let it die a natural death."

"And I was interested."

"Uh-huh. So then I was supposed to try and divert your interest. Jesus Christ, it was like a spy movie or something. You know—Mata Hari and all that jazz."

I said: "Divert my attention. And that accounts for your performance in bed, I imagine."

"You rotten bastard!"

"Well—"

"I was supposed to pump you, dammit. That's all. Then I was supposed to arrange a meeting with you for sometime the next day and stand you up. That way you would think I ran into trouble. It was supposed to make you forget all about Barb."

She was standing up now, her eyes fierce, her hands on her hips and her nostrils flaring. I told her to cool herself off. She thought it over, then sat down again.

"I slept with you because I wanted to," she said finally. "Take that and feed your ego with it if you want. I'm not a tramp. I've been around, I lead a full life for myself. I'm not a tramp. Don't call me one."

I looked at her. "Why did you come here tonight?"

"To talk to you."

"Why?"

"Because I think you can help me. Because I think we can help each other. I've already told you a few things, haven't I?"

"Nothing I hadn't guessed," I said. "Why did your play-mates give me a blackjack message?"

Her face darkened. "I'm sorry about that. I didn't know they were going to."

"How did the plans go?"

"They weren't too exact." She crossed one leg over the other, gave me a quick flash of thigh and a secret smile to accompany it. "I was supposed to stand you up last night. Then this morning or afternoon you'd get a phone call or a visit or something. A call from me or a visit from some of the boys. That would get you all wound up and you'd forget about Barb."

"Then the plans changed."

"Uh-huh. Hank called me this morning, Roy. He told me that Barb's roommate was knifed by that Al Marsten kook. That made it pretty obvious that you were going to get interested in Barb all over again. So I hurried back here."

I found my suitcase in my closet, opened it, took out what was left of the pint bottle of scotch the bellhop had brought me. I looked around for glasses and found none. There was probably a glass or two in the lavatory down the hall but I did not feel like going on an expedition. I opened the bottle and took a long drink straight from it.

"Don't I get any, Roy?"

"No," I said.

I took another drink, longer, and recapped the bottle. I unpacked my suitcase—since it looked as though I'd be around Cliff's End for a good time—and buried the bottle in a dresser drawer between a pair of white shirts. I turned to face her again, the scotch doing inexplicably magnificent things to my bloodstream.

I said: "It's a bloody shame."

"It is?"

"Yes."

"What is?"

"That you're not younger, or that I'm not older. You deserve a spanking, old girl. You should be turned over someone's knee and beaten to the point of tears."

"Me?"

"You. Did you happen to realize that you're up to your neck in at least one and probably two murders? Or didn't that occur to you?"

"What are you talking about?"

"I'm talking about murder. Barbara, for example. The suicide notion was foggy from the start. Now it's turning to pea soup, and thin soup at that. Dishwater, perhaps."

"You think she was killed?"

"Probably." I studied her. "And then there's Miss Davison, for that matter."

"But Alan—"

"—is sitting in a cell," I finished for her. "Accused of her murder. I don't think he's guilty."

"Then who is?"

"I don't know, I'm afraid. How does Hank Sutton look for the role? He's got a finger in all the other pies."

She thought it over elaborately. She tapped me for another cigarette, then managed to convince me that she deserved some of the scotch herself. I liberated the bottle from the dresser and passed it to her, watching her take it straight from the bottle without coughing or wrinkling up her pretty nose.

"That was a help," she said, returning the bottle. "I'd like to think Hank did it, Roy. I'd like to find a good reason to send him to the electric chair. Or watch somebody else send him. God, I hate that man!"

"But—?"

"But I can't believe it. Roy, when I talked to him on the phone this morning he was shocked. He couldn't believe it about Gwen, how it would have you back here on his neck and all. Why would he kill her? He was trying to let things cool down and that only stirred them up again."

She was right.

"Anyway, let's forget him for a minute," she said suddenly. "Don't you want to know why I came to see you?"

"I already know."

"You do?"

"Certainly," I said wryly. "You recently witnessed a murder. A man named Dautch—"

"Damn you, Roy!"

I laughed at her. "Now we're almost even," I said. "So you can tell me now."

"It's like this," she said. "Hank Sutton has those pictures. The negatives, anyway. And God knows how many prints he has of each of the pictures."

"Go on."

She went on. "I've been to his house, Roy. To deliver the money, of course. And before that . . . at the party."

"The photography session?"

She colored. "The photography session," she repeated. "Yes, I suppose you could call it that. Oh, you could call it

89

a lot of things, Roy. But to hell with it. Listen—I've been to his house. It's a big old place on the outskirts of Fort Mc-Nair and he lives there all by himself. He has . . . company, sometimes. I was his company once or twice, so I know. I told you about that, how he thought I was a lot of fun. An extra dividend in the blackmail game."

I nodded and wished she would come to whatever sort of point she was attempting to make. Hank Sutton lived alone in a large old house. But what did that have to do with anything?

"Those pictures are making everything a hell of a mess, Roy. If they were out of the way you might be able to get somewhere with your investigating. And the rest of the girls and I could take things easy, relax a little. It's horrible, knowing that there are pictures like that in existence. Sort of a photographic Sword of Damocles."

I was beginning to understand.

"It would be so simple, Roy. We would go there late after he was asleep. And we'd get inside the house and take the pictures away from him." Her eyes drilled into mine, radiating sweetness and warmth and innocence.

"You'll help me," she said. "We'll get them. Won't we, Roy?"

Nine

THE ROAD was a ribbon of moonlight and the red MG was a lunar rocket. And, while that particular imagery might have worried Alfred Noyes, it didn't bother me in the least. I had other far weightier considerations on my mind.

"Bear right," Jill was saying. "Then take the next left turn past the stoplight."

I nodded and went on driving. It was late—well after midnight, and I'd been up since four in the morning. It was almost late enough for me to behave like a bloody fool, and I was doing just that. We were on our way to the house where Hank Sutton lived. We were going to steal some dirty pictures from him.

The wisdom of this move was still lost on me, as it had been when Jill first suggested it. She'd had a properly difficult time selling the notion to me. But she was evidently a good saleswoman. We were headed for Sutton's house, ready to do or die, hearts set on securing the photographs once and for all.

It wasn't completely aimless, as I saw it. Jill herself was about as hard to figure out as a four-year-old's riddle, as transparent as a broken window. She wanted the photos back because she was tired of being blackmailed, tired of taking orders from New Hampshire's version of Al Capone. Her childish chatter about getting hold of the photographs in order to clear the air was a lot of bloody nonsense designed to make me think she was taking her stance on the side of the angels.

Still in all, she happened to be right—if for the wrong

reasons. The damned pictures cropped up no mater which way I turned around. In a sense they were the focal point of the entire case. As long as this Sutton individual had them in his possession, he would be tossing body blocks at me every step of the way.

But if we had them he might be out of the picture altogether. Perhaps that was too much to hope for, but at the least he would be subdued, with one major weapon taken away from him. It was vaguely analogous to nuclear disarmament; he might still start a war, but he couldn't do nearly so much damage.

And we were on our way.

"Turn right," she said. "Uh-huh. Now keep going straight ahead for three or four blocks. You're in Fort McNair now. Isn't it an exciting town?"

"Not particularly," I told her. It wasn't—very few tiny towns are especially exciting after midnight. This one was no exception, with its tree-shaded lanes and green-shuttered houses. It might be a fine place to live, but I'd hate to visit there.

"You're now almost out of Fort McNair, Roy."

"That was quick."

"Wasn't it? There's his house, on the other side of that open field. See it?"

I nodded.

"Open fields on every side. He likes peace and quiet. It should make everything easier for us, don't you think?"

I nodded again. I had slowed the car down and we were coasting in now. I pulled to a stop in front of the field she had mentioned and looked beyond it to Sutton's house. All the lights were out. There was a car in the driveway, a late-model Lincoln.

"He's home," she said. "That's his car, the only one he's got. So he's home."

"Asleep?"

"He must be. Or in bed, anyway. He might have a girl with him, Roy."

"Not with the lights out," I said.

"Why not?"

"Because you can't take pictures in the dark."

That made her blush a little. She turned off the blush, took out a cigarette and let me light it for her. "The front door's probably locked," she said. "How good are you with locks?"

"Fairly good."

"You're a talented guy, Roy. Okay, you go in the front door. The stairs are straight ahead, one flight of stairs up to the second floor. His bedroom's right at the landing."

"Bedroom?"

"That's where he keeps the pictures. He has them in this metal lockbox that he keeps under the bed. You can just take the whole box. You don't have to open it."

She was an amazing girl. I took another long look at the house and the car, then a shorter look at Jill. She was waiting for me to say something.

"That's all I have to do," I said. "Merely pick the lock, head up the stairs, sneak into the bedroom where he's either sleeping or making love to someone, crawl under the bed, grab the lockbox, and leave."

"Uh-huh."

I said: "You must be out of your mind."

"Can you think of a better way?"

I thought of a great many superior methods, such as turning the car around on the instant and driving directly back to Cliff's End. I suggested a few methods of this nature and she frowned at me. She looked extremely unhappy.

"You can do it," she said. "I told you he's all alone. Or he has a girl there, but she won't be any trouble. He's probably alone. He'll be asleep and you'll be awake. Why should you have a hard time with him?"

I asked her where she would be during all this fun and games. "I'll wait here for you," she said. "In the car. If anybody comes or anything I'll hit the horn and warn you. And when you come out of the house I'll scoot up in front with the car so you can just hop in. I know how to drive this buggy. Barb used to let me take it for a spin. I'm a good driver."

I told her that was reassuring. I got out of the car, leaving the keys with Jill. She slid easily behind the wheel and grinned at me. I went around to the trunk, opened it. There was a tool kit there, and in the tool kit I managed to locate a tire-iron. It seemed ideal for slamming Hank Sutton over the head, so I dropped it into a pocket and went around to Jill's window.

"Up the stairs and into the bedroom," she said. "The bedroom door's on the right of the landing. Don't forget."

"I won't."

"My hero," she said, only partially sarcastic. "My hero in baggy tweeds. Give me a kiss at parting."

I gave her a kiss at parting and she turned it into Penelope saying so-long to Ulysses. Her arms wound themselves around me neck and her tongue leaped halfway down my throat. When she let go of me there were stars in her eyes.

"Be careful," she said. "Be careful, Roy."

I was careful.

Very carefully I walked up the path to the house. I made my way up a trio of wooden steps that only creaked slightly. There was a door bell at the side of the door frame, and there was a knocker on the door itself, and I repressed a psychotic urge to ring bell and bang knocker and shout *Halloo!* at the top of my lungs.

I did not do this. Instead I fished in my pocket for my knife, a clever instrument made in Germany and equipped to perform every task from removing the hairs in one's nose to dissecting laboratory animals. It wouldn't cut a damned thing—the cutting blade wouldn't hold an edge to save itself. But it was excellent for opening locked doors.

The glass-paned storm door had a hook which dropped into an eye attachment screwed into the door-jamb. I slid the long cutting blade of the knife between the door and the jamb to lift the hook. This took care of the storm door.

The real door was heavy oak. It had two locks—a pin-tumbler type of spring lock and a supplementary bolt turned manually. I used the screwdriver blade of the knife to ease back the bolt, then sprang the spring lock with the cutting blade. I turned a brass knob and eased the door open slowly and gently. It opened without making a sound.

I looked into the darkness and listened carefully. The old house was silent as the grave and dark as a blackout in a Welsh coal mine. I stepped inside and drew the door shut behind me. A clock was ticking in one of the other rooms. I stood and listened to it, waiting for my eyes to grow accustomed to the darkness.

They did this a bit at a time. Gradually I became aware of the fact that the darkened interior of the house was not entirely black, that there were shapes and shades and shadows. A staircase loomed in front of me. I approached it, counted fourteen steps, and wondered how much the stairs would creak when I walked up them. Jill hadn't mentioned that point.

But they barely creaked at all. I walked up them like a man who had been riding horseback for several days without a pause, keeping my feet on the outward edges of the steps and being careful never to step in the middle of a plank. I stood without moving at the top of the stairs and wished for a cigarette, a long drink of scotch, and a seat in the parlor car of a fast train bound for New York. I dipped a hand into my pocket and drew forth the tire-iron. I hefted it in my hand. It was heavy.

I held onto the tire-iron with one hand, reached for the doorknob with the other. I turned it and heard the beginnings of metallic protest. It whined like a mosquito zeroing in for the kill. I took a deep breath and threw the door open. It made enough noise to wake the dead, and Hank Sutton was not even dead. He was very much alive.

He came out of sleep in a hurry. I saw the shadowy outline of his big body moving in the equally big bed. He swung both legs over the side of the bed and started to his feet.

"Who the hell—"

The room was completely dark, the shades all drawn. I moved from the doorway to one wall and pressed my back against it. He didn't know who I was or where I was and he couldn't see a thing. He hadn't moved.

"Okay," he snapped. "You're here, whoever you are. Why not turn on a light if we're gonna play games?"

I didn't answer. I heard the sound of a drawer opening, saw his hand move around by the tiny night table at the side of the bed. The hand came out of the drawer holding something that could only be a gun.

"To hell with you," he said. "You start talking fast or I blow a hole in your damned head."

But he was pointing the gun away from me, at the doorway. I took a deep breath and hoped he didn't hear me sucking air into my lungs. He had the gun and I had a tire-iron, and a gun can be a far more effective weapon than a tire-iron.

But I knew where he was. Which was even more of an advantage. I didn't have all the time in the world. At any moment his eyes would become aware of the fact that he was awake again, at which time he would be able to see. And once he could see, the fact that he couldn't hear me wouldn't make a world of difference. He would shoot a hole in my head just as he had promised.

"Come on, damn it! Who in—"

I rushed him.

I ran straight at him at top speed, with the tire-iron going up and coming down. The gun went off, rocking the room and filling it with the subtle stench of burning gunpowder. But the gun went off in the direction he had been aiming it, and that was not the direction I was coming from.

Then the tire-iron was curving down in a lovely arc, smashing all hell out of his wrist. The gun clattered from his hand and bounced around on the floor. I caromed into him while he roared like a gelded camel and held onto his wrist with his other hand. I bounced away from him—every action having an equal and opposite reaction—and wound up on the floor. Somewhere in the course of it all the tire-iron managed to lose itself.

"Son of a bitch," he howled. "What are you trying to do—kill me? You son of a bitch—"

I wasn't trying to kill him. I was trying to knock him colder than his pair of thugs had done for me in New York. I got to my feet and went for him. This time he saw me coming and threw a right at me.

It was a mistake. The punch landed but it hurt him more than it hurt me. He swung at me before he remembered what had happened to his wrist, and when his hand ran into my chest he howled again and fell backwards.

It was my turn. I hit him in the stomach with all my weight in back of the punch and he doubled up neatly. I crossed a right to his jaw and he straightened out again. He went back against a wall, then lowered his head and charged me as a wounded bull charges a matador.

He ran into a knee and fell flat on his face.

He wasn't moving. I picked up his head once or twice and banged it against the floor purely for sport. Then I went back to the doorway and rubbed one hand around the wall until my fingers found the lightswitch. I turned on lights and blinked—my eyes had grown completely accustomed to the darkness by then. I found a now-crumpled pack of cigarettes in my pocket, extracted a now-crumpled cigarette, and lighted it.

Hank Sutton was a big man. He had more hair on his chest than he had on his head. His nose must have been broken once and set poorly, and his wrist had been broken just recently by my tire-iron. He was stretched out on the floor and sleeping like a baby. I didn't even have to be careful not to wake him.

I looked under the bed and spotted the strong box. It was an ordinary gray steel affair about a foot long, six inches deep and four inches high. I reached under the bed and dragged it out. It had three circular tumblers with numbers on them from one to ten which constituted a sort of combination lock that wouldn't really keep a determined individual out of the box. I could have opened it in a moment or two but I didn't want to waste the time.

So I left him there. I picked up my tire-iron, tucked his .38 into the waistband of my trousers and his strongbox under one arm, and went down the flight of stairs in a hurry. This time I didn't bother stepping carefully, and this time each board that I hit squealed like a frightened mouse.

It was lovely—I had gone in there, smashed his wrist with a tire-iron, stolen a box of dirty pictures and taken his gun in the bargain. And the bloody fool didn't even know who I was! He hadn't so much as seen my face or heard my voice.

He was going to be unhappy. He was going to wake up with a quietly magnificent headache, with his blackmail material out the window and his gun along with it. I knew about the headache—his friends had given me one of my own in New York, and he had it coming. But the finest part of all was he wouldn't know who on earth had done it all to him.

Which was cute.

I got downstairs, tossed the front door open and went out through it. I saw the MG still parked in front of the field, and as I headed down the walk I heard her start the motor and head toward me. She slowed down long enough for me to get into my seat, then put the accelerator on the floor.

"Hey! Take it easy, girl."

She looked at me. "He'll be after us, Roy. He'll want to get that box back. He'll—"

"He's sleeping like a corpse."

"You didn't wake him?"

"I awakened him. Then I put him to sleep again."

"You . . . you killed him? Roy—"

The conversation was rapidly getting inane. So I told her to shut up for a moment, and then I told her what had happened, and then all at once the car was parked at the curb and the motor was off and she was in my arms, hugging me fiercely and telling me how wonderful I was.

It got involved.

Finally I said: "Hurry up and drive, Jill. It's late and we both have to get to bed."

"To bed? Why?"

"Because there's not enough room in an MG." I kissed her nose, her eyelids. "And you and I need a great deal of room."

"I know," she said softly. "I remember."

"Then start driving."

She shook her head stubbornly. "You're wrong," she said. "About what?"

"About there's no room in an MG. There's plenty of room. You never knew Barb Taft very well, did you?"

"Not very well."

She grinned. "Barb would never have owned a car if there wasn't enough room. See?"

I saw.

"Besides," she went on, "if I started driving now it would break the mood, and this is much too nice a mood to break. Don't you think so?"

"It's a fine mood."

"Uh-huh. And besides, I don't want to wait. All the way back to Cliff's End, for God's sake. And then trying to sneak into your moldy old room. I don't want to wait."

Her mouth nuzzled against my throat. Her body pressed hard against mine and her voice was a whisper of warmth.

"We can stay right here," she said. "And we can have a very enjoyable evening. I think."

And, as it turned out, she was correct.

Ten

I DROPPED her off at her dormitory despite her protests. She wanted to come with me, wanted to be on hand when I opened Sutton's strongbox, but I wouldn't listen to her. I explained that it was too damned late as it was, that I wanted to open the box in the privacy of my own room, and that sneaking her up Mrs. Lipton's stairs once in an evening was quite enough. She argued a bit and pouted a bit and finally accepted the state of affairs. She kissed me good-bye almost passionately enough to change my mind, then scampered off to her dormitory.

I drove back to Mrs. Lipton's, parked the car outside and carried the strongbox up to my room. It was the middle of the night, almost the middle of the morning, and soon false dawn would be painting boredom upon the face of the sky. I was exhausted and the bed beckoned.

So did the strongbox. I sat down on the edge of the bed with it and looked it over thoughtfully. The combination lock was a simple affair—three dials of numbers running from zero to nine, with a consequent nine hundred ninety-nine possibilities, the same as the odds in the policy slip racket.

I started spinning the dials aimlessly, trying to hit the right combination, then gave that up as fundamentally insane. Instead I took Hank Sutton's gun, hefted it by the barrel, and slammed the butt against the box.

It made a hellish noise. I sat still for a moment and felt guilty. I wondered how many boarders I had managed to awaken. Then I decided that one might as well wake them all and slammed the strongbox again with the gun.

This time it opened. I put the gun away in a drawer and opened the box. Its contents were no phenomenal surprise. First of all there were twelve negatives—two each of the six poses. I guessed that he was getting ready to pull the old gambit of selling the negatives for a high price, then resume the blackmail dodge. There were prints, too. Eighteen of them, three sets in all. All of them equally glossy, equally detailed, and equally pornographic.

I didn't waste time looking at them. I put them back in the box, adding the set I'd found in Gwen Davison's closet. Tomorrow I would have something to burn in a convenient field; for the time being only sleep interested me.

The strongbox—and the gun as well—went into a dresser drawer. While putting them away I came across what little remained of my bottle of scotch, and this could not have worked out more neatly if I had planned it. I finished the bottle and put myself, at very long last, to bed.

I was awake suddenly. It was noon and I was still tired but I'd had the magnificent luck to wake up tired or not. I sat on the edge of the bed and looked around for cigarettes. There didn't seem to be any.

It was that sort of day. There are days when one bounces out of bed filled with life and easy of spirit. There are other days when one wakes up coated with a fine layer of foul sweat, and on those days that sweat seems to have seeped into one's brain. And it was that sort of day. My brain felt sweaty.

I shook my head to clear it, then shuffled down the hall to the community bathroom. Someone was in it. I went back to my room and shifted uncomfortably until someone got out, then took his or her place. The shower was either too hot or too cold all the while I was under it, the spray either too hard or too soft. I struggled with the controls only for a small while. On days like that, you cannot fight with fate. You do not stand a solitary chance of success.

The towel provided might have blotted a small puddle of ink. It wouldn't do for a full-sized human being. I did as much as I could with it, then trundled back to my room and waited for the water to evaporate. I had a strong urge to roll around in the rug but managed to control myself.

One of *those* days.

I got dressed and dragged myself out of the house. The cold spell had broken, which should have been a pleasant turn, but it was the wrong day to expect pleasant turns. Rain had come with the warm air, rain that mingled with the fallen snow and made slush out of it. In New York you learn to accept slush as part of the winter wonderland environment. In New Hampshire you expect a little better in the way of weather.

I squished through the slush to the MG and wondered if it would refuse to start. But the gods smiled and the engine turned over. I drove over to the main street of town and parked the car.

The drugstore didn't have any of my brand of cigarettes left. I should have expected as much. I settled for a pack of something else, then went next door and smoked a cigarette while a waitress brought me orange juice and toast and coffee. There was nothing wrong with the orange juice, but the toast was burnt and the girl put cream in the coffee.

Which was par for the course.

I ate the toast without complaining, had her trade the cup of dishwater for a cup of black coffee, and smoked my way through the day's second cigarette. Then I sat there for a few moments wondering what was going to happen next. Something, no doubt. Something abominable.

So I left the lunch counter and went to the police station. And it happened.

I asked the old policeman if I could talk to Alan Marsten. He stared at me. "You mean you ain't heard?"

"Heard what?"

"About the kid," he said. "About what he did, the Marsten kid."

"I didn't hear anything," I said mildly.

"No?"

"I was sleeping," I said patiently. "I just awoke."

"Ayeh," he said. "Sleeping till noon, eh? You private police have the right deal, by God. Sleeping till noon!"

We had the right deal, by God. I wondered if they would

throw me in jail for hitting the old fool in his fat stomach. I decided they probably would.

"The Marsten boy," I reminded him.

"Escaped."

"What!"

He smiled with relish. "Escaped, I said. Run off, took to the woods, disappeared."

"When? How? What—"

"Hang on," he said. "One at a time. First the *when* part. Happened about three hours ago, just after I come on duty. Then the *how*—that lawyer of his came in to see him. I opened the door and the kid gave me a hit over the head that was enough to put me out on the floor. When I came to he was gone. They say he ran out, jumped in a car that some damn fool left the keys in. And off he went like a bat out of hell."

I must have had a magnificently foolish expression on my face because he was smiling patronizingly at me. "The lawyer," I managed to say. "What about the lawyer?"

"Kid hit him. Hit him same as he hit me, with one of the legs he busted off that little chair in his cell. The lawyer was still out cold by the time I got up."

There was probably little enough that was even mildly humorous about it, but it came at the right time, on top of no cigarettes and burnt toast and coffee with cream in it, on top of an occupied shower and a feeling of ill-being and everything else that went along with it. The mental picture of that fine Philadelphia lawyer tapped on the head with a chair leg was too much for me.

I laughed. I howled like a hyena, clutching my belly with one hand and pawing the air with the other. I roared and whooped hysterically while the excuse for a policeman watched me as if I had lost my mind. Maybe I had.

The laughter stopped almost as suddenly as it had started. I straightened up and tried to get my dignity back. "No one knows where he was headed?"

"Nope."

"Or why he ran off?"

"Hell," he said. "Guess that's easy enough. He figgered he

103

better run away before we hang him. He's guilty as hell and he wants to save his neck."

I didn't believe it. The more the situation developed, the more little puzzle-pieces started to come into view, the less likely it seemed for Alan Marsten to have killed Gwen Davison. After what I'd learned in the past day he was bloody well coming into the clear. I was all ready to suggest releasing the boy, when the little fool decided to set himself free.

"We'll get him," the cop assured me. "You know what they say—he can run but he can't hide. Dumbest thing a man could do, running away like a rabbit the way he did. That way not a soul in the world's going to believe he didn't cut that girl to pieces."

He dropped me a sly wink. "More'n that, I don't figger his lawyer's going to love him. Not going to work too hard to get him off. The boy really let him have it with that chair leg, let me tell you. By God, that fancy talker had a lump on his head the size of a turkey egg!"

He had a lump on his own head. It was more the size of a duck egg, as it happened, but I decided against mentioning it to him. He probably already knew.

Instead I thanked him, for nothing in particular, and left him there. I went out into the slush again and used the butt of one cigarette to get a fresh one started.

On the way to where the MG was parked I ran into Bill Piersall, the younger and somewhat more competent Cliff's End police officer. He told me what the other one either hadn't known or hadn't thought worth mentioning. The car Alan Marsten picked was a dark blue Pontiac, three years old, with New Hampshire plates. The state troopers already had word of the jailbreak plus descriptions of boy and car, and they were in the process of throwing a roadblock around the area.

Which, according to Piersall, was not a difficult procedure. "Just a few roads out of here," he explained. "They can seal 'em all off in no time at all. That boy's caught in a net, Mr. Markham. He can't get far."

"What if he stays in town?"

He looked at me blankly. "Why'd he do that? He's a dead

104

duck if he stays around. Why, he just about admitted his guilt by taking off like that. He stays around and he doesn't have the chance of a fish in the desert."

"Perhaps," I said. "But he might be safer trying to hide out. Especially with the roads sealed."

He nodded thoughtfully. "We'll check," he assured me. "We'll give the town a good going-over, see if we can't turn him out. But I think he'll be off and running, Mr. Markham. I think they'll pick him up on Route Seventeen heading south, as a matter of fact. He's running scared, you see. Might be safer for him, trying to hide, but he won't stop to think on that. He busted out of that cell because he was scared and he'll run for the same reason."

He was on his way to the station house. I let him go and got into the red MG, fitted the key into the ignition and started the motor running. Piersall's analysis was intelligent enough, I thought, but it was probably wrong.

If I was right, Alan hadn't killed Gwen Davison. And, in that case, he wasn't running away out of fear. He was running in an attempt to accomplish something, to find somebody, to perform one task or another. And if that were so, he wouldn't be leaving Cliff's End. He'd either go straight for whomever it was he wanted to see, or he'd hide out and wait for things to clear up.

That was the way it appeared to me. Which, taking into consideration the way the day had gone thus far, indicated that Piersall was probably right. Alan was a killer on the run and they'd pick him up at the roadblock on Route 17.

It was that kind of a day. But it has to be a hellishly bad day before I'll stop playing out my own hunches. And things weren't quite that bad yet.

Not quite.

I drove back to my home away from home first of all. Those photographs were still around, and as long as they remained in existence they were a potential weapon for anybody who had his hands on them. As far as that went, I didn't know whether or not Mrs. Lipton made it a practice of going through her guest's drawers simply out of curiosity. I didn't want her to get an eyeful.

I parked the car and went into the large tourist home. Mrs.

Lipton met me with a smile and asked me if I would be staying another night. I smiled back at her, told her I probably would, and paid her for another evening. She held the smile while she pocketed the bills, then stepped out of my way and let me go up the stairs, taking them two at a time. I went into my room and closed the door after me.

The strongbox was in the drawer and the pictures and negatives were in the strongbox. I carried the box to the lavatory, locked myself in, and tore each of the eighteen photos into tiny and innocuous shreds. I did the same for one strip of six negatives, but I changed my mind and folded the other strip, putting it into my wallet. There was always the chance that the photos might come in handy at a later date. Even if they didn't, I could always make prints and sell them to high school children if the going got rough.

I flushed the shredded prints and negatives down the bowl, unlocked the door and left the bathroom for whoever might want it. I put the broken strongbox back in my drawer because there wasn't much else to do with it, tucked the gun back into the waistband of my trousers. God knew what use I might have for it, but it could conceivably come in handy.

Back in the MG again, I sat for a moment feeling like a yo-yo top on a string, bouncing back and forth all over the town of Cliff's End and accomplishing nothing at all. Thoughts like that can only depress one. I got the car going again and drove off.

Jill wasn't in her dormitory. A hallmate told me she had classes from one to three that afternoon, then usually dropped over to the college coffee shop for a bite to eat. I left a note on her desk to the effect that I would meet her at the coffee shop after three on the chance that she returned directly to her room. I looked at my watch—it was one-thirty, which gave me an hour and a half to kill before I could see her. I looked for a way to kill it.

Helen MacIlhenny was one way. I found the dean in her office, evidently not too busy to see me. I sat down in a chair and looked across her desk at the woman. She asked me if I was getting anywhere and I told her the truth.

"A few dozen things are happening," I said. "But no pattern's developed yet. Maybe I've accomplished nothing. It's hard to say."

"Are you piling up clues?"

I smiled sadly. "It doesn't work that way in real life," I said. "Only in the comic books. You pick up a piece here and a piece there and you never know which are clues and which are trivia. Then the final piece drops into place and everything works itself out. It's fun when it's over, but a headache while it's going on." I turned the sad smile into a grin. "A headache some of the time, anyway."

"Meaning now, I suppose?"

"Meaning now."

She nodded. "Is there anything I can do for you, Mr. Markham? Anything I can tell you?"

"Maybe. Is there anything on the order of a curfew for the students here? A bed check or something of the sort?"

"Freshmen have to be in their dormitories by midnight, two o'clock on weekends. It's strictly enforced."

"And the older girls?"

"No curfew," she said. "We have a rather liberal philosophy of education at Radbourne, Mr. Markham. We believe that you have to give a student responsibility in order to teach him to handle it. A bed check or curfew would be rather inconsistent with that way of thinking."

"It would. Is attendance required at classes?"

"Only the first and last class of each session. If a student is going to acquire knowledge, he or she will do so out of motivation, not compulsion. Class attendance is not required. Some students learn the material as well on their own. And, to be painfully frank, some of our lecturers aren't worth getting up at eight in the morning to listen to. As the students are well enough aware, Mr. Markham."

I nodded. "Then it would be possible for a student to leave campus for a day or two without anyone realizing it."

"Oh," she said. "You mean Barbara—"

"Not specifically."

"Oh," she said again. "Yes, I would be inclined to say that it's possible enough, Mr. Markham. A student could go away and return without it coming to my attention, or to the attention of anyone in authority. Of course, a prolonged absence would not go unrecognized. Barbara's case is a case in point. Some students worried about her and called the matter to my attention."

She thought for a moment. "And a prolonged absence would not be disregarded," she went on. "There's no hard and fast rule against it, you understand. But it would be discouraged."

I didn't say anything. I was not thinking about Barbara Taft at the moment. As a matter of fact, I was clearing up Jill Lincoln's trip to New York, among other things. I looked at Helen MacIlhenny. She had a thoughtful expression on her face.

"Mr. Markham," she said, "I have the feeling that you know something which I don't know."

"That's not likely, is it?"

Her sharp eyes twinkled. "Oh, I'm afraid it's highly likely. You ought to tell me. I'm supposed to have my finger on the pulse of Radbourne, so to speak. The dean must know all that goes on around this little campus."

"So must the detective," I said.

"Then you don't have anything to tell me? I've a feeling something has been going on behind my back, something serious. And that it's linked with the murder."

I admitted that it was possible. "When I have something," I said, "I'll let you know about it."

"Will you?"

"Of course."

"I wonder if you will, Mr. Markham."

There was a pregnant pause. It was my turn to ask her something so I picked up my cue.

"What do you know about a girl named Jill Lincoln?"

"Jill Lincoln? Why?"

I tried to be nonchalant. "Someone mentioned her as a close friend of Barbara's," I said. "I may be having a talk with her soon to find out if she knows anything. I like to know something about a person before a conference."

"Is that all?"

"Certainly."

She looked quizzically at me. "Oh, well," she said. "I suspect you'll tell me what you want to and when you want to, and I suspect that's your privilege. What do you want to know about her?"

"Whatever you feel is pertinent."

"I see. Well, there's not much to say, I'm afraid. I've never had much contact with the girl, Mr. Markham. She's a reasonably competent student and she's never been in any serious trouble, the sort that has to be brought to a dean's attention."

"From a wealthy family?"

"Why do you think that?"

"I don't know." I shrugged. "Barbara seems to have had friends from the upper circle, so to speak."

Helen MacIlhenny frowned at me. "Radbourne's liberalism is a social affair as well, Mr. Markham. There's remarkably little grouping along dollar lines. As a matter of fact, Jill's family is not too well off at all, hardly in a class with Barbara's. Her father owns two or three dry-goods stores, as I understand it. He's no candidate for the poorhouse, not by any stretch of the imagination. Devoutly middle-class—that might be a good way to put it. No, Jill doesn't come from wealthy parents."

On the way to the police station I stopped in the drugstore, took up temporary residence in the telephone booth and put through a call to the Taft home in Bedford Hills. Edgar Taft wasn't in but Marianne was.

She took the call.

"Roy," she said, "I was hoping you would call. Now, while Edgar was out."

"Something happen?"

"No," she said. "Nothing's happened, not really. But I wanted to tell you that . . . that you don't have to waste any more time up in Cliff's End. You can come back to New York now any time you feel like it."

"Really? Is that Edgar's idea?"

She hesitated. "Not . . . exactly. Roy. I appreciate what you've done. He was very upset emotionally by Barb's death; you know that. You've been a settling influence. Otherwise he would have sat around feeling that nothing was

109

being done, and he's a man who cannot live with that feeling."

She stopped, probably for breath. I waited for her to get back on the track.

"But now I think he has accepted the fact that Barb committed suicide, Roy. I've . . . I've tried to help him reach that conclusion. His attitude has been a common one. He thinks of suicide as a cowardly act, the act of a worthless person. But I've been making him . . . I should say helping him . . . to realize that Barb was a very sick girl, an extremely distrubed girl. And that can make a difference. He sees that now."

I let her wait for an answer until I had a fresh cigarette going. Then I said: "So now he's cooled off and I'm supposed to drop everything. Is that the idea?"

"More or less."

"I see. Marianne—"

"You could come to New York, Roy. Come up to our place this evening, talk to Edgar, tell him you've been working like a dog and nothing's turned up to indicate anything but suicide. Then tell him that as far as the reason for her depression goes, it seems as though it'll be impossible to determine it for sure. Tell him it was just one of those unfortunate things, that—"

"Marianne."

She stopped.

"I can write my own dialogue, Marianne. I don't need a script, you know."

"I'm sorry," she said.

"I'm afraid I'll be in Cliff's End another day or so at the least. Not solely because of your daughter's death. I'm involved in another matter as well."

"In Cliff's End?"

"That's right."

A significant pause. "I see, Roy. Well, all right. I just thought that the sooner he could be reassured once and for all that Barbara wasn't murdered. Well, you'll be back soon enough, I suppose."

"I suppose so."

"Yes," she said. "Roy, I want you to know how much I

110

appreciate everything you've done so far. It means a great deal both to Edgar and to myself."

I didn't answer.

"When Edgar comes home, should I give him any message? Or I could call his office if it's anything important. He doesn't like it when I disturb him during office hours—"

"I thought he was retired."

A slight laugh. "Oh, you know Edgar. He'd lose his mind without an office. Roy, is there anything you want me to tell him? Any message?"

"No," I said. "There's no message."

I put the phone on the hook and wondered why something bothered me. I should have felt relaxed enough. I did not.

Alan Marsten. I had to get to the police station and find out what, if anything, had happened. Piersall had his theory, that the boy would be caught at a roadblock, and if it were true he had probably been caught already.

If not, I wanted to find him.

Because if Piersall was wrong and I was right, then Alan Marsten was on his way somewhere, looking for somebody, ready to do something. Somebody might get hurt—either Alan or the person he was looking for.

Who would he be after? Why had he run—like a rabbit or like a lion, depending upon your point of view—and what in the name of the Lord was he planning?

Good questions.

Then I thought of an answer . . .

Eleven

BILL PIERSALL had lost most of the forest-ranger look. He sat behind his desk now, a cup of black coffee at his elbow, the receiver of a phone pressed to one ear and gripped tightly in one hand, a cigarette burning itself out between the second and third fingers of the other hand. As far as the phone conversation went, he seemed to be doing more listening than talking. I stood in front of his desk, ignoring his waving signals to sit down and relax. Instead I shifted impatiently from one foot to the other and waited for him to finish up.

He did, finally. He cursed somewhat boyishly and set the receiver in its cradle, then fastened weary eyes on me.

"Nothing so far," he said. "Not a damn thing."

"No action with the roadblocks?"

"Oh, we've had action in spades," he said bitterly. "Three suspects hauled in so far and none of 'em looked any more like that Al Marsten than you or me. One of 'em was thirty-six—can you imagine that? Thirty-six years old and madder than hell to be pulled in like a crook, and ready to sue the whole damn state of New Hampshire for false arrest."

He picked up the coffee cup and drank most of what was in it. He put the cup down and made a face. "Cold," he explained. "Even the coffee's cold in this godforsaken state."

"You've had nothing then?"

"Nothing." He finished his cold coffee and screwed up his face once more in disgust. "Looks like you're right," he said, not too grudgingly. "Must be he's hiding out in town. Not even a native could get through those roadblocks, and he's no native. He doesn't know the country at all."

112

"Where are the blocks?"

"One's down on Seventeen between here and Jamison Falls. That's where I thought we'd get him. And there's a few—"

"How about Sixty-eight? Is the road blocked?"

"Sure."

"This side of Fort McNair?"

He was shaking his head. "Other side," he said. "Sixty-Eight's the only road through McNair so they might as well close it further down to make sure he didn't get there before 'em. What's happening in McNair?"

"I'm not sure," I said. "But I think we'll find Alan Marsten there."

"You know something?"

"I might. Want to help me take a look?"

"Right!"

He was up and around the desk like a shot. He dropped the cigarette to the floor and covered it with his foot. Then the two of us were out of the building.

"My car's by the corner—"

"We'll take mine," I said. "It moves faster."

We piled ourselves into the MG. I noticed the gun on his hip on the way and remembered that I had a gun of my own, on my own hip. His was in a holster while mine was tucked under my belt.

I wondered if we'd be using them.

I got the MG going and gave the engine its head. The car picked up quickly and scooted over the road.

"Some car," Piersall said.

"It's a good one."

He was laughing and I looked at him. "Just thinking," he said. "Just struck me. Wouldn't it be hell if some dumb son of a bitch of a trooper stopped us for speeding? Wouldn't it be the thing?"

"Don't worry," I said. "They couldn't catch us."

I put the accelerator pedal all the way to the floor and left it there.

"Hank Sutton," I said. "Know anything about him?"

We were hitting the outskirts of McNair and I let the MG

113

slow down a bit. The weather was beginning to clear up. I remembered how the weather had matched the miserable mood of the early part of the day. I wondered if the improvement was supposed to be an omen.

"I know he's a son of a bitch."

"Is that all?"

"Nope," he said. "I know he runs everything crooked in this part of the state. And that a lot of people would like to see him in a cell. Or with a rope around his neck. He lives in McNair, doesn't he?"

"Yes."

"That where we're going?"

"Yes."

"I'll be a son of a bitch," Bill Piersall said. "I'll be a ring-tailed son of a bitch."

There was something totally disarming about the way he swore. It was almost embarrassing, as it is when you overhear a maiden aunt use a dirty word. It seemed improper, a betrayal of the Scout Law or something of the sort.

"We going up against Sutton?"

"Probably. He's in this up to his ears."

"In what?"

"This Marsten mess."

"Didn't Marsten kill the gal?"

"No."

"Son of a bitch," he said. "Who did? Sutton?"

I said: "I don't know who killed her. But now Sutton's going to kill Marsten. Maybe."

"I don't get it," he said, puzzled. I told him that I really didn't get it myself, not entirely, and that we'd both know a lot more about it in a short enough span of time. This didn't really satisfy him but it left him without any questions to ask. So he stopped asking questions.

Either I remembered the route Jill and I had taken the night before or the car knew the way all by itself. Whichever was the case, I made the right turns and did the right sort of driving until, all at once, we hit the other side of McNair and Sutton's large and ancient house came into view. There it was on the other side of the field in front of which Jill had waited just the night before.

We didn't wait by the field. I pulled the car right into the driveway and hit the brakes hard. We stopped dead just a few feet from the rear of Sutton's big Lincoln. It was still where it had been the night before.

And a blue Pontiac was parked in front of the house.

"He's here! I'll be a son of a—"

But we were in motion before he could get the word "bitch" spoken. We got out of the car and started moving automatically. He was heading for the house's side door while I went around in front.

"I'd like to get that bastard," he said. "That Sutton bastard. He's big but he's not too big to take down a peg."

"Well, he's inside."

"Yep," he said. "Maybe he'll come out."

He shouted: "Open up, Sutton! Police!"

There was no answer. I tried the door; it was locked. I didn't bother playing childish games with my German knife this time. I aimed Sutton's gun at Sutton's lock and squeezed the trigger. There was an appropriately impressive noise and the smell of burning wood. Then I kicked the door and it swung open.

Piersall was at my side suddenly. Evidently he'd decided to give up the side door approach and join me at the front. He shouted at Sutton again. There was no answer.

We went inside to the vestibule, guns still drawn. I looked up at the flight of stairs that I'd gone up so slowly and silently the night before.

Then I saw motion. I grabbed Piersall and gave him a shove and dove myself for the floor.

A gun went off and a bullet went over our heads.

We crouched on either side of the vestibule archway. Sutton was in the bedroom at the head of the stairs, the room where I had halfway knocked his head in just twelve or thirteen hours ago. He couldn't come down and we couldn't go up.

"Must be another staircase," Piersall was saying. "I'll go around, see what I can do."

I shook my head. "No other stairs," I said. "Not in a house like this one. There's this staircase and that's all. He's stuck up there and we're stuck down here."

"We can wait him out. Call back for help, starve him out."
He scratched his head. "Maybe have them drag up some
tear gas. That gets 'em every time."

"On television?" He looked sheepish and I felt ashamed
of myself. "Anyway, he's got the boy. Alan Marsten. He
may still be alive but he won't be unless we get him in a
hurry."

"How?"

It was a bloody good question. On the surface it looked as
much like a stalemate situation as anything had ever looked.
But there had to be an answer. There were two of us and
there was only one of Sutton.

And that should make some sort of difference, a difference
in our favor. Two to one is fine odds.

I peered carefully through the archway. His gun went off
again and I jerked back. The bullet was a foot off and it still
seemed too close.

"He's got us shut up tight," Piersall said. "And we got him
shut up just as tight."

I tried to remember back to the night before. Something
about his room—

"There's a porch in back," I said. "An upstairs porch off
the bedroom, a sort of small balcony."

"There is, huh? You sure?"

"You can see it from the road," I lied.

"Didn't notice it," he said. "What do you figure?"

"You stay here," I told him. "Don't let him get out of that
bedroom. Take a shot at him every few minutes to keep him
sitting up there. I'll see what I can do."

"You going up on that porch?"

"I may."

He whistled soundlessly. "That's a neat trick," he whispered. "If he sees you coming—"

"Then I'm dead."

"You said it. Sure you don't want to wait him out?"

"We'd wait all day. I'd rather take the chance."

I took a pot shot at Hank Sutton's doorway and let the
noise of the gunfire cover me while I scurried out of the
house like a frightened rabbit. Then I went through the driveway and alongside the house to the back yard. There was a

116

porch off the bedroom. Incredibly enough, you *could* see it from the road.

The garage contained everything on God's good earth, with the singular exception of a ladder. I looked around for a ladder until I was convinced it wasn't there, then backtracked to the house itself again. The garbage cans were arranged in a neat row by the side of the cellar door. If I could haul one close to the porch without Sutton hearing me, and if I could stand on it and reach the porch—

And if wishes were horses.

I hadn't seen many beggars riding recently. None but Alan Marsten, and he had come riding in someone else's car. If wishes were Pontiacs—

I found one of the garbage cans, the only one not filled with garbage of one sort or another. I picked it up, first setting the lid in the snow, and carried it over close to the porch. Then I inverted it so that I'd have a surface to stand on and set it down.

It made noise. But at that precise moment one of the men inside the house shot at the other man, and that covered the comparatively small sound of the garbage can. I managed to climb up on top of it, again making a small amount of noise that no one seemed to notice.

Now I could reach the porch.

I found a convenient pocket and dropped Sutton's gun into it, hoping it wouldn't go off while I was climbing and shoot a hole in my leg. I reached up and took hold of the edge of the porch floor with both hands, then got one hand onto a bar in the wooden railing. I hoisted myself up partway and saw that I'd gauged things badly. I was climbing up directly in front of the door that opened out onto the porch. If he looked around he would see me. And if he saw me, he would be looking at the world's most beautiful target since the invention of the bull's-eye. I had both hands on the damned railing, and if I let go I'd fall on my face.

But there were compensations. This way at least I had the ability to see inside of the bedroom. I took a good look.

Sutton had his back to me. I saw the gun in one of his big hands. He was by the door, ready to squeeze off another shot at Piersall.

Then I saw Alan.

He was not much to look at. He was crumpled up by the foot of the bed and it was impossible to tell whether he was alive or dead. I saw bloodstains—or what looked like them— on the rug. It seemed logical to assume the blood was Alan's.

I pulled hard with both hands and raised myself a few more feet. I reached for the top of the railing, took hold of it and wondered how strong it was. It was evidently strong enough. I placed both feet on the outer edge of the porch floor and prepared to step over the railing.

A gun went off and I almost fell down again. Sutton jerked his head back—evidently Piersall had squeezed off another shot at him.

I drew a breath. Then I drew my gun, taking it from my pocket and letting my index finger curl around the trigger. I wanted him alive, but it might be hard that way.

I looked at Sutton. He still hadn't turned toward me, which was ideal. I hoped he wouldn't.

I succeeded in getting one foot over the rail. I started to bring the other one over to keep it company, then stopped in the middle of the act and poised there like a ballet dancer in the fifth position.

Because Alan Marsten moaned.

The sound was barely audible through the porch door, but it must have been clear enough to Hank Sutton. I stood there posing prettily while he turned around in the direction of the moan. I brought up the gun to cover him.

But he didn't see me. He was looking at Alan.

Then he turned the gun on Alan. And I realized at once that he was going to eliminate this moaning nuisance, that he was going to shoot Alan dead.

I yelled: "Sutton!"

He whirled at the noise and his gun came up fast, away from the boy and pointed straight at me. I must have fired at about the same time he did, because I heard only one noise. A bullet snapped through the glass door and whined over my shoulder. Another bullet—one of mine—snapped through the door and took him in the center of his big barrel chest.

He grunted. He took one reluctant step backward, and

then a big ham of a hand came up to grope around that hole in his chest. It did not do him any good. He backed up again —just a half-step this time—and then reversed his direction, pitching forward onto his face.

And there I was, with one foot on either side of the railing. I reacted very slowly now, almost numb. I picked up the retarded foot and promoted it, lifting it ever-so-gently and leading it over the railing. The porch door was locked so I shot the lock off for the sheer joy of it. The bloody gun was a toy now and I was a child playing games.

I went to the head of the stairs and called for Piersall.

Sutton was stone cold dead. We rolled him over and checked his pulse. We put a shard of broken glass from the porch door first to his nose and then to his mouth. There was no pulse, no heartbeat, and no breath frosted the shard of glass. We let go of him and he fell back down again, staring at the ceiling through empty eyes.

"Pretty shooting," Piersall said admiringly. "He was going to shoot you, eh?"

"He tried. He was getting ready to put a bullet in the boy. To get him out of the way, I'd guess."

That reminded us that there was a third person in the room. We turned to Alan. He was conscious, after a fashion. But he had obviously taken a rugged beating. One eye had been hammered shut and his face was caked with blood from nose and mouth. He was missing an occasional tooth and it was an odds-on wager that a few of his ribs were dented.

He said: "—had the pictures."

I listened to him. We had to get him to a hospital in a hurry, but first I wanted to get everything he had to tell me.

"Thought . . . thought I took them. I didn't. Came after him to get them. But—"

He stopped, tried to catch his breath by sucking huge mouthfuls of air into his lungs. His good eye closed for a moment, then managed to open.

He said: "Bastard."

And that was the extent of his conversation. He closed

119

his good eye again and quietly passed out. I decided it was his privilege. I didn't blame him a bit.

"This kid's got to go to a hospital," Piersall said. "He took a beating."

"I know. Is there one nearby?"

"Five miles down the road. Want to give me a hand with him? We better be careful—he'll have broken ribs and God alone knows what else. We don't want to make him any worse than he is already, the poor son of a bitch."

We each took an arm and managed to get Alan to his feet. We walked him over to the stairway, then got him downstairs a slow step at a time.

"Be a son of a bitch," Piersall said again. The swearing was beginning to sound somewhat more natural now. He was growing into it.

"Got to give that kid credit," he said. "He went up against a bastard, all right. Sutton can take most anybody. Could, that is. Guess he can't take anybody now, can he?"

"I guess not."

"That was pretty shooting," he told me again. "I was just a damn fifth wheel, wasn't I? Sitting safe and cozy while you went and climbed right up after him."

"One of us had to stay there."

"Yeah," he said. "I guess." He bit his lip. "But that was sure nice shooting."

We carried Alan out of the house and down the walk. He was still unconscious and I hoped he would stay that way until he was in the hospital where a needle of morphine would make things easier for him. Sutton was a professional, and nobody can hand out a beating the way a professional can.

"Hell," Piersall said. "How we gonna do it?"

"Do what?"

"Take him there," he said. "Only room for one in that damn MG. One plus a driver, I mean. We can't stick him in the trunk, can we?"

We rather obviously couldn't.

"Suppose we could take him in the Pontiac," he said doubtfully. "But it's going to be cute enough at the roadblock as she stands. Some of those troopers don't know me. They'll give us a hard time if they see the Pontiac."

"Take the MG."

"Just me and him?"

"That's the idea," I said. "It moves faster, for one thing. For another, you don't need me along. And you can strap him in with the safety belt. That will keep him in place."

"I never drove one of these," he said. Then he grinned hugely. "It'll be fun trying, I guess. She got a regular H shift or what?"

I explained that there were three forward speeds and showed him where each gear was. Then we loaded the still-unconscious form of Alan Marsten into the right-hand seat and strapped him securely in place.

Piersall settled himself behind the wheel. He played around with the gearshift lever until he figured it out for himself, then turned to look at me.

"How'll you get back to town?"

"In the Pontiac or the Lincoln. One or the other."

"Good luck," he said. "That was sure some action we had, wasn't it?"

"It was."

"We don't get much of that around here," he said. "It's mostly a quiet town, quiet part of the country. I hardly ever shot a gun before in what they call the course of duty. Warning shots now and then, that kind of thing. But never shooting to kill."

"A little excitement never hurts," I said.

"Yeah. Well, I'm glad somebody finally got to Sutton. He was a son of a bitch, a real live son of a bitch. And now he's a dead one."

He started the MG, put her in low and drove away. I watched him until he was out of sight, then walked over to the Pontiac. The keys were not in the ignition.

I swore softly, then checked the Lincoln. No keys.

I went back into Hank Sutton's house, tugged a lamp loose from the wall socket and cut off a length of wire. I stripped the ends with my knife, carried the wire to the Lincoln and pretended I was an all-American juvenile delinquent running a hot wire on a car for a joy ride around the block.

If I had to hot-wire a car, it might as well be the Lincoln. Not only was it more fun to drive, but the Pontiac was a car the police would be looking for. I didn't want to be stopped.

I remembered what to do and did it. Amazingly enough it worked. The engine turned over and I put the Lincoln in reverse and backed out of the driveway. After the MG, the Lincoln was bulky and awkward, an oversize and overweight bundle of metallic nerves.

But on the highway it loosened up and showed me what a nice clean motor it had. I pointed the car toward Cliff's End and glanced at my watch. It was only a quarter to three, and it didn't seem possible.

I was going to be on time for our date.

Twelve

THE RADBOURNE coffee shop was a cold gray room in the basement of the student lounge. A cluster of tables—round ones seating eight and square ones seating four—gleamed of formica here and there around the room. Students drank coffee, sipped unidentifiable beverages through straws, munched cheeseburgers and talked noisily, and incessantly.

I looked around for Jill and didn't find her. I went to the counter, bought a cup of coffee, and carried it to an empty table. I sat down and lighted a cigarette while I waited for the coffee to cool. And for Jill to arrive.

At a table not far from mine a young man and a girl sat eating ice cream. The boy was the all-American type—crew cut, broad forehead, boat neck sweater, khaki trousers, an intelligent-but-unimaginative expression on his face. The girl was quietly pretty, with light brown hair and rosy-apple cheeks. There was something naggingly familiar about her, and yet I was certain we had never met.

Then I realized just what it was that was so naggingly familiar, and I looked away guiltily. She was familiar, certainly. I had seen her picture.

And in that picture she had not looked nearly so wholesome.

I tried the coffee. It was still too hot and I sat the cup back in its saucer and took another deeper drag on my cigarette. I looked at my watch. It was after three, and Jill was due any minute.

I wondered how Alan Marsten was. He'd taken a hell of a beating, a professional job of punishment quite professionally administered. But he was a game lad. Game enough to knock out a pair of men in order to escape from his jail cell. Game enough to go up against a heavyweight type like Hank Sutton. All of which made him very game indeed.

I hoped he'd be all right.

Now Alan was in a hospital, mending, and Sutton was in his own house, lying dead and growing cold and stiff. And I was waiting for a pretty girl to come and drink a cup of coffee with me, and wondering when in God's name she'd arrive.

She arrived, ultimately. It was almost three-thirty when she walked in the door, her hair neatly combed, her expression alert. She was carrying a leather notebook under one arm and was wearing a loose gabardine coat over a heavy sweater and a pair of plaid slacks.

I saw her before she saw me. She stood up straight and surveyed the room with sharp eyes, looking everywhere but at me. Then finally she saw me and headed over to my table. She dropped herself heavily into the chair directly across from me and slammed her briefcase quite dramatically upon the table. Her cheeks were pink from the cold and her eyes were bright.

"Hi, Roy."

"Hi."

"I got your note," she said. "You wanted to see me."

"That's right."

"How come?"

"To talk."

A heavy mock sigh. "That's disappointing," she said. "That's disappointing as hell."

"It is?"

"Uh-huh."

"Why?"

"Because," she whispered, "I thought maybe you wanted to make love to me. But all you want to do is talk. And that, kind sir, is disappointing."

She stood up again. "Not that I'm unwilling to talk," she said. "But first my system demands coffee. Wait here, Roy.

I'll be back as soon as I convince the idiot behind the counter to sell me a mug of mud."

I watched her walk to the counter, her full hips swaying ever so slightly under the coat. I tried my coffee again, and this time it was drinkable. Jill came back, her coffee cooled and polluted by cream and sugar. She sat down again and asked me for a cigarette. I gave her one. As she leaned forward to take the light I held for her I could smell the perfume of her hair. I looked at her, and I remembered the night before, and another night not too long before that.

She said: "Hello, you."

I didn't say anything.

"Hey! Did you hear about Alan?"

"What about him?"

"He broke out of jail," she said. "Isn't that just one for the books?"

"I heard."

"One for the books," she repeated. "I don't know exactly what happened—I heard it fourth or fifth or maybe tenth-hand. But he hit his own lawyer and slugged a cop and stole a car and ran out of town."

I told her that was substantially what had happened. Her eyes narrowed.

"Then that cinches it," she said. "Sort of kills your theory, too."

"My theory?"

"That he was innocent. He wouldn't bust out of jail if he was innocent, would he?"

I didn't answer.

"He must have killed Gwen," she said. "It probably broke him up when Barb killed herself—I guess he was more deeply involved with her than anybody realized. And he knew Barb and Gwen never got along very well. So that probably set him off. Made him want to get revenge, if you see what I mean. As if Gwen had anything to do with what happened to Barb."

I nodded thoughtfully.

"It's kind of nutty," she said. "But he's kind of a nut. He always has been—you know, a little weird. Something like

125

Barb's death could set him off and make him go nuts all the way."

I picked up my cup of coffee and drained it, then set down the empty cup in the saucer. I looked up at the clock on the wall, looked over at the lunch counter. I was very tired now, tired of murders, tired of violence, tired of the college of Radbourne and the town of Cliff's End and the whole bloody state of New Hampshire. I wanted to go someplace far more civilized and get disgustingly drunk.

I said: "Marsten has been found."

She stared. "You're kidding!"

"I'm serious."

"But . . . oh, that's impossible! Roy, you let me babble on and on about him and he's already been found. You're terrible, did you know that? But tell me about it, Roy. Where was he? Who found him? What happened?"

I drew a breath. "I stopped by the police station on the way over here," I told her. "They couldn't tell me too much. They'd just received a phone call a moment or two ago from the state troopers. They found Marsten in a town a few miles north of here. They didn't tell me which town, but I don't suppose it matters."

I watched her face very carefully. "He seems to have gone berserk," I went on. "They found a man there whom Marsten had murdered. Then the boy put a gun in his mouth and blew his brains out. Murder followed by suicide."

She tried to keep the relief from showing in her face. She was a rather accomplished actress but she was not quite good enough. Her mouth frowned but her eyes could not help dancing happily.

She said: "What on earth—"

"Some neighbors called the police," I said. "When they heard the gunshots. It seems that Marsten broke into this man's home in order to use his place to hide out. Evidently the man resisted in one way or the other and our boy didn't like that. Alan had a gun—God alone knows where he found it—and he shot the man.

"Then I suppose he suddenly realized just what he had done. He'd killed Gwen Davison and had murdered an in-

126

nocent man, and the two acts were too much for him. So he killed himself, and that's the end of it."

Now the relief was obvious. She was one happy little girl now. She drank more coffee, finishing her cup, and flicked ashes into it from her cigarette.

"Then I was right," she said.

"Evidently."

"Well," she said. "That clears up your job, doesn't it? You can tell Barb's folks she committed suicide, but don't tell them about the pictures—it would only make them feel bad. And Gwen's murder is all solved now." She smiled. "And I'm off Hank Sutton's blackmail hook, thanks to you. You did me quite a favor last night, Roy. Quite a favor."

I didn't say anything.

"Poor Barb," Jill Lincoln said. "Poor kid—if she had just kept a good grip on herself everything would have been all right. I tried to tell her just to hang on, to keep paying off Sutton until we found a way to stop him once and for all. But she was a pretty mixed-up kid, Roy. And that was enough to push her over the edge."

"It's a shame, isn't it?"

She nodded sadly. "Poor Barb," she said again. "And poor Gwen, getting killed almost by accident. And poor Alan and that poor man who got in his way. It must have been terrible for Alan, Roy. That one horrible moment when the curtain lifted and he realized what he had done. And then killing himself."

She lowered her eyes and studied the table-top. I reached across the table and covered her hand with my own.

"Come on," I said. "Let's get out of here."

"Where do you want to go?"

"Some private place. Any suggestions?"

She though it over. "I guess my room's okay."

"In your dormitory?"

"Uh-huh."

"Am I allowed in there?"

"During the day you are. Let's go."

We got up from our chairs and walked out of the coffee shop. She tucked her leather notebook under one arm and buttoned up her gabardine coat. As we left the building she took my arm.

"Where's your car, Roy?"

"I left it downtown. We can walk to your dorm, can't we? It's not far."

We walked to her dormitory. I'd left Sutton's Lincoln parked a short way down the block, but her dormitory was in the other direction and we did not pass the big car. I was glad of that. It was an uncommon sort of car, and I suspect she might have recognized it.

We went into her building, climbed stairs to her floor, walked down the hall and into her room. Her roommate was not in. Jill tossed her notebook onto a bed, then turned to close the door of the room.

"Now watch this part closely," she said.

I watched closely. She rummaged around on the top of her dresser until she managed to locate a hair pin. Then she returned to the door and did something with the hair pin. She turned to me triumphantly and beamed.

"See?"

I didn't see.

"Come here," she said. "I'll show you."

I came and she pointed. I looked while she explained. "I drilled a little hole through the gizmo that keeps the door shut," she said. "and when you stick a pin in, it locks the door. You aren't allowed to padlock the doors or anything, but this works perfectly. Now nobody can get in, not while the pin is in place. It's perfect."

I told her it was amazing to what lengths college students would go to secure privacy. I told her the mechanism she had devised was ingenious. Then she threw her arms around my neck and kissed me. It was the typical Jill Lincoln kiss, the sort that tickles one's tonsils.

"Privacy," she said. "You Tarzan. Me Jane. That—" pointing "—bed."

I managed to smile.

"Oh, damn it," she said.

"Damn what?"

"Just *it*. You'll be going back to New York now, won't you? I mean, the case is all bottled up or bundled up or whatever it is a detective does with cases. You won't be able to stay here and dally with me much more."

"That's true."

"Am I fun to dally with, Roy?"

"Great fun."

She grinned. "You don't dally so badly yourself, kind sir. Maybe I can get down to New York every so often. Maybe we can do a little more dallying."

"Maybe."

She stepped forward again, ready to be kissed, and even now I wanted to take her in my arms and kiss her, hold her, make lovely love to her. The personal magnetism of the girl was extraordinary. Even now, knowing what I knew, with all the puzzle fragments securely locked in place and the whole ugly picture revealed, the girl managed to be charming and exciting.

But I stepped back. Her eyes studied mine and, perhaps, saw something there. She waited for me to say something.

"You're very pretty, Jill."

"Why, thank you—"

"You're very pretty," I repeated. "Have your lawyer get a great preponderance of men upon the jury, dear. That way you won't hang. You'll go to prison for a very long time, but you won't hang."

She stared at me. She had grown very secure now, and was perfectly happy about everything, and my words were coming out of left field.

"Because you killed Gwen."

Her jaw fell.

"That's right," I said. "You killed her. Alan Marsten let Barb borrow his knife. She must have given it to you. And you killed Gwen with it."

"Is this supposed to be a joke, Roy? Because it's not very funny."

"It's no joke."

"You really think I—"

"Yes. I really think you killed her."

She stood stock still for a moment, nodding her head slowly to herself. Then she turned around, walked to the bed, sat down on it. She picked up her leather notebook and toyed with the zipper, her eyes on me.

She said: "You're out of your mind, you know."

"I don't think so."

"Really?"

"Really."

"Then pull up a chair," she said, her voice acid. "Sit down and tell me all about it. This ought to be interesting. Did I have any particular reason for killing Gwen?"

"Yes. She was fouling your blackmail operation and you were afraid you'd find yourself in trouble."

Her eyes went as wide as tea-cups. "My blackmail . . . oh, you're kidding."

I pulled up a chair near the bed and sat down. "It was a very pretty set-up," I said. "I have to grant you that. I guessed that someone was on the inside, that Sutton couldn't have worked it out all by himself. You gave me a quick story about Sutton being a pick-up of Barb's, told me the rest of you went along to the party for the lark. But that didn't add up.

"An operation like this one needed preparation," I went on. "Someone had to pick the right girls, had to have enough of their confidence to get them to the party in Fort McNair. The girls had to have money, for one thing. No one would be fool enough to blackmail the average college girl for anything more than her maidenhead. The average college girl gets a few dollars a week and no more. But the girls in your little group were good subjects for blackmail, weren't they?"

She did not answer. She was still playing with the zipper on the notebook, running it back and forth, avoiding my eyes with her own eyes.

I went on. "At first I thought Gwen was the inside girl. It seemed logical enough at the time—she resented Barbara Taft's wealth, and when I found the photographs in her closet I thought she was in on the operation. That notion had me wandering around in circles. I couldn't get anywhere with it.

"It was much more logical to figure it the way it actually happened, Jill. One of the girls being blackmailed wasn't really being blackmailed at all. She was on the inside, setting things up and taking her cut of the profits. And she was always above suspicion as far as the blackmail victims were concerned. They thought she was in the same boat they were in. They never realized she had set them up for Hank Sutton."

"And I'm the girl?"

"Yes."

"Why? Why me?"

"Several reasons," I told her. "First of all, you were the pauper of the group. Barb certainly wouldn't have been a blackmailer, not with the funds at her disposal. I thought of that possibility, as a matter of fact, but it didn't make much sense. Dean MacIlhenny told me this afternoon that you don't have much money at all, Jill. You act rich and you dress expensively, but your father hasn't much money. It had to come from somewhere."

She didn't say anything.

"And you were the girl Sutton used to run his errands; you admitted that much on your own. You came to New York to set me off the trail. You collected the blackmail money for him. You knew where his house was and had been there often enough to have the layout committed to memory. My God, you even knew where he stashed the negatives! He wouldn't tell you that if you were on his hook —it wouldn't do him any good. But as his partner, you had a certain right to know."

She was gnawing at her lower lip. I could see her trying to figure out a way into the clear. She hadn't been able to find one yet.

"Let me tell you what happened, Jill. You arranged things and they were working splendidly. Then Barbara Taft disappeared and you started to worry. I came to Cliff's End looking for her and you worried a little bit more, enough to tell Sutton all about it. He wasn't even around campus; he never would have known I was investigating. But you were here and you found out."

"Then what happened, Roy?"

"Then you followed me back to New York," I said. "You had Sutton phone friends of his in New York and arrange

131

for a pair of parties. His friends chased us in the cab so that you could pump me for information. Then they let us get away and I stashed you in an apartment in the Village."

"Where we made love."

I ignored that. "You left early in the morning," I went on. "You caught the first train back to Radbourne and left me to get my head knocked in by more of Sutton's friends. You told me the other day that you came back here when Gwen was killed. That was a lie, Jill. You came back right away, figuring I was confused enough for the time being. Then you killed Gwen."

"Why would I kill her?" She was smiling now but the smile didn't quite bring itself off. "I was trying to throw you off the trail, remember? Why do something to increase your suspicion and bring you up here again?"

"Because you couldn't help it."

"Why not?"

"Because Gwen found Barb's set of photographs," I told her. "She recognized your picture and called you up."

"So I killed her because she was going to blackmail me? Don't talk like a moron, Roy. I was a blackmailer myself, remember? And I didn't have any money, so she couldn't blackmail me, of course. So that knocks your theory—"

"She wasn't blackmailing you."

"No?"

"She wasn't a blackmailer," I went on. "She was the sort of girl who believed in playing everything by the book. She came across the photographs, had enough sense to realize that somebody was being blackmailed with them, and decided to go to the authorities. But first she wanted to find out what she could about it. She called you over, told you what she was going to do, and probably asked you if you would go to the police with her."

I lighted a cigarette. I blew a cloud of smoke at the ceiling and sighed.

"And you got panicky, Jill. You had the knife with you and you used it. Or you told her not to do anything until you had a chance to talk with her at length, then returned that night and knifed her with Alan Marsten's knife. That sounds more likely, come to think of it.

"You see, Alan couldn't have slipped in and out of a girl's dormitory at that hour without attracting attention. He couldn't have gotten close enough to kill her without her screaming. But you could, Jill. And you did. She was expecting you and she was hardly afraid of you. You killed her and left her there and walked out with no one giving you a second glance."

"Roy—"

"Hold on," I said. "And sit still, dear. You're getting a little nervous just about now, aren't you? Let's not make any sudden moves. I want you to listen to this all the way through."

She stopped fidgeting and looked at me levelly. Even now it was more than a bit difficult for me to believe that everything I was saying was true. She looked like a sweet and demure college girl.

Not like a blackmailer.

Or a murderess.

"Then I came along again," I said. "You hated like hell to let me know who you were, but you couldn't help yourself. For two reasons—I would probably find out anyway if I poked around long enough. And more important, you needed a little help. As long as Sutton had those photographs, you were in trouble. He could work the blackmail game and it could backfire, with you getting hurt. Or he could start blackmailing you, as far as that went.

"But with Sutton out of the picture one way or another, he couldn't do much of anything. So you sent me after him to get the pictures, figuring that one of three things could happen. He could kill me, in which case at least I was out of your hair. Or I could kill him, in which case everything was every bit as perfect. Even better.

"Or I could get the pictures—which is what happened, of course. That helped. There was still more."

She looked at me. "Oh, tell me," she said, the sarcasm a bitter edge to her words. "Tell me everything, dear Roy. Don't make me guess."

I said: "I dropped you at your dorm last night. Then I went home to sleep and you came outside again. Do you want me to tell you where you went?"

"Of course."

"You went to the police station. Oh, you didn't go inside, because that would have been senseless. You went around the rear and banged on Alan's window. You awoke him and fed him a story, a long story about how a man named Hank Sutton had been responsible for Barbara's death in one way or the other. I don't know what you said—maybe that he was blackmailing her and she killed herself, maybe that he actually murdered her. It doesn't really matter. Whatever it was, it was enough to set him off like a bomb. He broke jail and went after Sutton."

"Why did I do that?"

"Because you thought it could only help you. If Sutton killed Alan, then Alan would be forever tagged with Gwen's murder. Everyone would reason that an innocent boy wouldn't escape from a jail cell.

"And if Alan killed Sutton, that was just as good as far as you were concerned. Alan would hang, certainly, and Sutton would be out of the way."

"Really?"

"Really."

"Well," she said. "Well, they're both dead, aren't they? So it worked out perfectly. And with them both dead you'll have a hard time convincing anybody that there's any truth in this little fantasy of yours, won't you?"

I just smiled.

"Well? Won't you?"

I said: "Alan Marsten might help me out."

"But he's dead!" Her eyes were wide again. "God damn it, you said he was dead!"

"So I lied," I said. "You can sue me."

She lowered her eyes again and we sat there in silence. She unzipped the leather notebook all the way a little at a time, her fingers nervous.

I told her what had happened, how Bill Piersall and I had managed to get to Sutton's house, how I had shot Sutton dead, how Alan was already at the hospital recovering.

"Then I'll tell the police about you," I said. "And if they don't believe me, he can help out with an appropriate word here and there. And then do you know what will happen?"

"What?"

"Then you'll go to jail," I said. "And you'll stand trial for murder. You'll be found guilty. But I don't think you'll hang, not with enough men on the jury. You'll wind up in prison for life. With good behavior you'll be out in twenty or thirty years or so."

"Roy—"

"What?"

She decided not to answer. I wondered why she kept fooling around with the leather notebook. She was dipping one hand into it when I caught on.

I dove for her. By the time I got to her there was a gun in her hand but she just was not fast enough. I hit the gun with one hand and her jaw with the other. The gun flew against a wall and went off aimlessly, a bullet plowing into the ceiling. Plaster showered down on us.

I stood up shakily. She sat up even more shakily, rubbing her jaw where I had hit her with one hand. The game was up now and she recognized the fact. Her eyes held a beaten look. She was giving up.

And then all Hades was breaking loose. The gunshot attracted a certain amount of attention, with half the female population of Radbourne banging on our door and wondering what was wrong. And the door, of course, was locked. Her hair pin held it securely in place.

I walked over to pick up the gun. I kept it trained on her and back to the door, pulling out and discarding the hair pin. I opened the door and turned to the first girl I saw.

Then Jill was yelling. "He tried to rape me! Call the police; he tried to rape me!"

The girl looked at me.

"Call the police," I told her. "By all means. I want them to arrest Jill for murder."

"Murder?"

"Gwen Davison's murder. Hurry, will you!"

The girl looked at me, at Jill, at me again. Jill went on shouting something foolish about rape while I ignored her manfully. The girl nodded to me, then went off to find a policeman.

135

I walked toward Jill again. Her eyes were dull now. She'd made one last-ditch attempt, a final round of desperation, and it had not worked.

"You didn't have a chance," I said.

"No?"

"No. Nobody could rape you, Jill."

"Why not?"

"Because you'd never resist," I said.

Then I sat down in the chair again and kept the gun pointed at her while we waited for the police to come.

Thirteen

It ended at the Tafts', at dinner.

Dinner was sandwiches and beer this time, and none of us were very hungry. Jill Lincoln was in jail in New Hampshire, charged with the murder of Gwen Davison. Alan Marsten was in a hospital recuperating. Hank Sutton was in a morgue, decomposing. Barbara Taft was dead and buried.

During dinner I did the talking and Edgar and Marianne listened in silence. Painful silence. I said the things I had to say and they listened, because they had to listen, certainly not because they wanted to.

Edgar Taft stood up, finally.

"Then she really did kill herself, Roy."

"I'm afraid she did," I said.

"It doesn't play any other way, does it?"

"No."

He nodded heavily. "You'll excuse me," he said. "I'd like to be alone for a few moments."

Marianne and I sat there awkwardly while he left the room and went to his study. She looked at me and I looked back at her. I waited.

"I'm sorry you had to tell him," she said.

"That it was suicide?"

"The rest of it, Roy. Those . . . those pictures. That filth. All of it."

"It would come out in Jill's trial anyway."

"I know. But it seems so—"

She let the sentence trail off unfinished. I took a cigarette from my pack, lighted it, offered her one. She shook her head and I blew out the match and dropped it into an ashtray.

"You didn't want me to tell him about the pictures," I said. "Is that it?"

"It's just that—"

"But you knew about them all along," I said, interrupting her. "Didn't you, Marianne?"

Her hands shook. "You knew," she said. "You *knew*—"

"Yes," I said. "I knew. I knew that you knew, if that's what you mean. There was a reason for Barbara coming to New York to commit suicide, Marianne. Because that's not why she came here. She came to see her mother."

She had closed her eyes. Her face was very pale.

"Blackmail bothered her," I continued. "She didn't like being bleeded even if she could afford the money. She didn't like letting some filthy crook hold a filthy picture over her head like a sword. They say you cannot blackmail a truly brave person, Marianne. I suspect there's quite a good deal of truth in that statement. And I suspect that Barbara was a very brave girl."

"Brave but foolish, Roy."

"Maybe." I sighed. "She was brave enough to want to call a blackmailer's bluff. She was confused as hell—she left school, dropped out of sight for awhile, then came home. She came to you, Marianne. Didn't she."

She said: "Yes." The word was barely audible. It was more a breath than a word.

"She wanted support," I went on. "She told you about the pictures and the blackmail. She told you she was going to tell the man to go to hell, then tell the police what he was doing. She knew there was going to be publicity, and that it would be the worst kind—she would be asked to leave school, perhaps, and there would be nasty rumors."

"It would have been bad for her, Roy. A reputation around her neck for life. It—"

"So you told her to go on paying. You probably were harsh with her, although that hardly matters. What mattered to Barbara was that her mother wouldn't back her up, that her mother seemed to be more interested in appearances than in reality. That ruined her, Marianne. Her own mother wouldn't support her. Her own mother let her down."

"I never thought she would kill herself, Roy."

"I know that."

"I never thought . . . I was horrible with her, Roy. But it seemed more sensible to pay the money than to risk the publicity. I didn't take anything else into consideration. I—"

She broke off. We sat there, awkward again. I finished my cigarette.

"That's why you didn't want me to work too hard on the case," I said. "That's why you told me on the phone to drop it as quickly as I could. You thought I might turn up the pictures, and you didn't want that."

"It would have hurt Edgar."

"It's hurting him now," I said. "But Barbara's death hurt him a great deal more."

She said nothing.

"I'm sorry, Marianne."

"Roy—"

I looked at her.

"You won't . . . tell Edgar, will you?"

Appearances were everything. She still lived in a little world of What Other People Think, and reality was not rearing its ugly head, not if she could help it. She was poised and polished as a figurine. And as substantial.

"No," I said. "Of course not."

The train transported me to Grand Central Station. I walked to the Commodore, reclaimed my key from the clerk, picked up bills and messages. I took an elevator to my room and put the bills and messages into a drawer without looking at them.

I took off my coat, my jacket, my tie. I could hear Christmas carols coming from somewhere. I wished they would stop. Christmas was coming any day now and I didn't care.

I picked up the telephone, called Room Service. I asked the answering voice to send up some scotch. I told him to

139

forget about the ice and the soda, and to make it a fifth, not a pint.

I sat down to wait for the liquor. The Christmas carols were still going on and I tried not to listen to them.

It was the wrong night for them.

MYSTERY / SUSPENSE
AVAILABLE FROM CARROLL & GRAF

☐ Eberhart, Mignon G. / Message from Hong Kong	3.95
☐ Gardner, Erle Stanley / Dead Man's Letters	4.50
☐ Gilbert, Michael / The Crack in the Teacup	3.95
☐ Gilbert, Michael / Roller Coaster	4.95
☐ Kitchin, C. H. B. / Death of His Uncle	3.95
☐ Kitchin, C. H. B. / Death of My Aunt	3.50
☐ Lansdale, Joe R. / Act of Love	4.95
☐ Lansdale, Joe R. / The Nightrunners	4.95
☐ Millhiser, Marlys / Willing Hostage	4.95
☐ Muller, Marcia and Bill Pronzini / Beyond the Grave	3.95
☐ Muller, Marcia and Bill Pronzini / The Lighthouse	4.50
☐ Pronzini, Bill / Dead Run	3.95
☐ Pronzini, Bill / Snowbound	4.95
☐ Reid, Robert Sims / The Red Corvette	4.50
☐ Sandra Scoppettone / A Creative Kind of Killer	4.50
☐ Sandra Scoppettone / Donato & Daughter	6.95
☐ Sandra Scoppettone / Razzamatazz	4.95
☐ Sandra Scoppettone / Some Unknown Person	5.95
☐ Stevens, Shane / The Anvil Chorus	4.95
☐ Stevens, Shane / By Reason of Insanity	5.95
☐ Stevens, Shane / Dead City	4.95
☐ Stout, Rex / A Prize for Princes	4.95
☐ Stout, Rex / Under the Andes	4.95
☐ Symons, Julian / Bogue's Fortune	3.95
☐ Waugh, Hillary / A Death in a Town	3.95
☐ Willeford, Charles / The Woman Chaser	3.95

Available from fine bookstores everywhere or use this coupon for ordering.

Carroll & Graf Publishers, Inc., 260 Fifth Avenue, N.Y., N.Y. 10001

Please send me the books I have checked above. I am enclosing $_____ (please add $1.75 per title to cover postage and handling.) Send check or money order—no cash or C.O.D.'s please. N.Y. residents please add 8¼% sales tax.

Mr/Mrs/Ms _____

Address _____

City_____ State/Zip_____

Please allow four to six weeks for delivery.